POST-MORTEM EVIDENCE

Borgo Press Books by S. Fowler Wright

Arresting Delia: An Inspector Cleveland Classic Crime Novel
The Attic Murder: An Inspector Combridge and Mr. Jellipot Classic Crime Novel
The Bell Street Murders: An Inspector Combridge and Mr. Jellipot Classic Crime Novel
Black Widow: A Classic Crime Novel
The Capone Caper: Mr. Jellipot vs. the King of Crime: A Classic Crime Novel
Crime & Co.: An Inspector Cleveland Classic Crime Novel
Dawn: A Novel of Global Warming
Dead by Saturday: An Inspector Cleveland Classic Crime Novel
The End of the Mildew Gang: An Inspector Cauldron Classic Crime Novel (Mildew Gang #3)
Four Callers in Razor Street: An Inspector Combridge and Mr. Jellipot Classic Crime Novel
The Hanging of Constance Hillier: An Inspector Cleveland Classic Crime Novel
The Jordans Murder: An Inspector Combridge and Mr. Jellipot Classic Crime Novel
The King Against Anne Bickerton: A Classic Crime Novel
The Mildew Gang: An Inspector Cauldron Classic Crime Novel (Mildew Gang #1)
Murder in Bethnal Square: An Inspector Combridge and Mr. Jellipot Classic Crime Novel
The Police and the Public
Post-Mortem Evidence: An Inspector Combridge and Mr. Jellipot Classic Crime Novel
The Return of the Mildew Gang: An Inspector Cauldron Classic Crime Novel (Mildew Gang #2)
The Rissole Mystery: An Inspector Combridge and Mr. Jellipot Classic Crime Novel
The Screaming Lake: A Lost Race Novel
The Secret of the Screen: An Inspector Combridge and Mr. Jellipot Classic Crime Novel
Three Witnesses: A Classic Crime Novel
Too Much for Mr. Jellipot: An Inspector Combridge and Mr. Jellipot Classic Crime Novel
The Vengeance of Gwa: A Fantasy of Prehistory
Was Murder Done? A Classic Crime Novel
Who Murdered Reynard? A Classic Crime Novel
The Wills of Jane Kanwhistle: An Inspector Combridge and Mr. Jellipot Classic Crime Novel
With Cause Enough?: An Inspector Combridge and Mr. Jellipot Classic Crime Novel

POST-MORTEM EVIDENCE

AN INSPECTOR COMBRIDGE AND MR. JELLIPOT CLASSIC CRIME NOVEL

by

S. FOWLER WRIGHT

WRITING AS "SYDNEY FOWLER"

The Borgo Press
An Imprint of Wildside Press LLC

MMVIII

CONTENTS

POST-MORTEM EVIDENCE

CHAPTER I.

"I WANT you to understand, Mr. Jellipot, that this is a quite unofficial visit," Inspector Combridge said, as he sat down.

"Yes, yes, of course," the solicitor answered. "Always glad to see you, Inspector." His thought was: "He wouldn't say that, if it were no more than a friendly call." But they were old friends, with a mutual confidence in each other's discretion, and if Inspector Combridge chose to preface whatever he might have to say in that manner, it was not Mr. Jellipot's disposition to challenge it.

"The fact is, I've recommended a client to you, and I'm not sure that you'll thank me for what I've done."

"If you've arrested anyone," Mr. Jellipot said cautiously, "of whose guilt you are less than sure, I should be unlikely to refuse to do anything in my power—"

"I haven't arrested anyone," the inspector answered, with some natural irritation, the reply inevitably bringing recollection of the recent Attic Murder case to his mind,[1] when he had been unfortunate enough to put two innocent persons, one after the other, into the dock, before Mr. Jellipot's diffident but acute assistance had enabled him to snap handcuffs upon the guilty man. "I haven't arrested anyone, and I don't know that there'll be any occasion to do so. I don't arrest people unless I have got really good grounds for concluding that I am putting them where they ought to be; and I shouldn't be likely to arrest anyone and ask you to get them off in the same breath."

"No," Mr. Jellipot agreed thoughtfully, without appearing to notice the irritation he had aroused, "I can see that. It isn't likely you would."

After saying this, he remained silent, waiting for his visitor to continue, and Inspector Combridge controlled his momentary an-

---

[1] See *The Attic Murder*.

noyance to ask, in a friendlier voice: "I expect you've read something of the Hamilton case?"

"No, I can't say that I have. I suppose it's some criminal matter that's in the Press? But *The Times* Law Reports are about all that I get time to look at most days now."

"Well, you wouldn't see it mentioned in them. Not yet, anyway. And there really hasn't been much published, nor much happened as yet.

"Mrs. Hamilton was a wealthy widow, who lived at East Grinstead. Her only companion, beside the domestic staff, was a step-daughter, Ada Hamilton. Mrs. Hamilton was an elderly lady with that indefinite complaint a weak heart, and Ada nursed her.

"She had no children of her own, and her husband had left his estate tied up, so that she had the income—a matter of about two thousand pounds yearly—for life, with reversion to his daughter by an earlier marriage—the Ada I've mentioned.

"Mrs. Hamilton died about three weeks ago. Her doctor certified the cause of death without showing any hesitation, and she was buried in the ordinary course.

"But on the day she was buried the coroner had an anonymous letter. It came too late for him to stop the interment, even had he been of a mind to do so on no better evidence, but he had a consultation subsequently with Mrs. Hamilton's medical attendant, Dr. Burfoot—quite a good man, by the way—and after that he applied to the Home Office for an exhumation order."

"Which, of course, he got?"

"Yes. There was no difficulty. The relatives raised no objection, and of course it wouldn't have made much difference if they had, unless to draw suspicion upon themselves. But in fact Ada—the only one closely concerned—appeared to think it a good idea. That's the one point in her favour."

"Then you are going to tell me that she is accused of poisoning her stepmother?"

"Not at all. If anyone did poison her, I should say that there wouldn't be much doubt as to who it was, but we don't know that she's been poisoned at all. The adjourned inquest's on Friday morning, and Sir Lionel Tipshift's to have his report ready by then."

"You've no idea what it's likely to be?"

"Not the least. Sir Lionel very properly deferred the autopsy until Dr. Burfoot could be present, and I understand that the result of an analysis of some of the internal organs won't be known till tomorrow afternoon."

"But I suppose you may often get a hint of what it's most likely to be?"

"Yes. Sometimes we do. But in this case Sir Lionel Tipshift and Dr. Burfoot say the same thing, that it's better to be dumb till they're quite sure."

"That sounds reasonable," Mr. Jellipot suggested.

"Yes. They evidently agreed upon it after the first examination was made. It's an attitude you can take either way."

"Yes, so you can. But what is it you want me to do, if that's how the case stands, and who for?"

"Miss Ada Hamilton asked me to recommend her to a good solicitor. She wants to find out who wrote the anonymous letter."

"Well, it seems a sensible step to take. But it's not quite in my line. I'm not a detective agency."

"No. I suppose you'd instruct a suitable office, if you take the thing up at all."

"Probably I should. I suppose the coroner's got the letter now?"

"Yes, it's his property. But you could inspect. There'd be no difficulty about that."

"What sort does Miss Hamilton appear to be?"

Inspector Combridge hesitated. "She may be quite a respectable young woman. She's not my style. She doesn't look like a murderess, or talk like one for that matter, but then I never knew one who did."

"And you have known several?" Mr. Jellipot enquired, checking the value of the inspector's evidence with his usual precision.

Inspector Combridge observed the implication of this question without offence. He replied, after consideration: "Yes, four—only one that we were able to hang, but the others were quite as sure."

"Then you can speak with more than common experience.... The young lady was able to influence you sufficiently for you to recommend her to me?"

The inspector received this with rather less complaisance than the implication which he had answered previously. He said: "Well, I like to be fair. And I thought I could put her on to you better while there's no accusation against her than I might afterward.... Besides, it can't hurt us to know who wrote the letter, whether it were well founded or not. Rather the other way."

"Yes, I see that. By the way, it sounds like the kind of investigation that will require out-of-pocket payments. Has Miss Hamilton any means of her own?"

"I understand that she comes into her father's estate, now that her stepfather's dead. I don't know beyond that."

"But if she murdered her stepmother she wouldn't benefit under that will."

"No, I suppose not."

"Well, I'll do what I can if she comes to me."

Mr. Jellipot said this without enthusiasm, and Inspector Combridge, feeling no certainty of the wisdom of what he had done, got up to go.

CHAPTER II.

THE inspector was halfway to the door when Mr. Jellipot delayed him with a further question.

"By the way, to whose benefit would it be if Ada Hamilton should lose her rights under her father's will? I mean, do you happen to know who is the next heir?"

"Not certainly. There's a cousin, Vincent, who'd probably benefit more or less. I don't know whether there may be anyone nearer than he."

"You don't connect him with it, anyway?"

"No, I rather wish that I could."

There was a tone of bitterness in the inspector's voice which Mr. Jellipot was not likely to pass unremarked.

"It sounds," he said, "as though you have met him before."

"So I have. As a matter of fact, I'm the one man living who can give him a clean bill of innocence in this matter. If there were any foul play about Mrs. Hamilton's death, he's about the only man in England of whom I can swear to my certain knowledge that he wasn't concerned. You see I had him under observation at the time in connection with a different charge."

"Something you can't tell me now?"

"I don't see why I shouldn't. We had information laid against him for obtaining money by false pretences. It was one of those cases which no reasonable person could doubt, but which fell short of what you lawyers call proof. For about a fortnight I shadowed him everywhere that he went, trying to pick up the missing link in the chain, and I've got a record of his every movement when he was outside his own bedroom, and every telephone call that he made, or which was put through to him."

"That," Mr. Jellipot considered, "may prove to be very important to him, if there should have been a crime, and he be an innocent man."

"So it may; though it wasn't exactly the object I had in view. But I don't suppose you'd care to hear the whole tale. It's a bit long, and you looked busy when I came in."

"So I was," Mr. Jellipot admitted, "and every minute that I spend talking with you means that I shall have to work later tonight; but if I'm to take a case up at all, I like to know as much as I can about the people concerned; so if your own time will allow—"

"Well, you can have it for what it's worth. But as to it having any connection with Mrs. Hamilton's death, you'll understand, when you hear, that there's none at all. Its only importance is that it shows that Vincent wasn't concerned.

"The first I heard of it was when the landlord of the Rolfe Hotel came to us at Scotland Yard and said he'd been done out of five hundred pounds, and would the Public Prosecutor take it in hand?

"The Rolfe is a medium-class hotel near Victoria Station. We've nothing against it, or the landlord—Wall his name is, Nicholas Wall—except that it's mostly patronized by bookmakers and sporting men of the louder type.

"Wall's tale was that Vincent Hamilton had been staying at his hotel for about six weeks. He had been introduced by a regular customer, a man named Baildon, who admitted it, and appeared to have acted in good faith. There's nothing known against Baildon, and all he said about Vincent seems to have been from his own knowledge, and to have been substantially true.

"Vincent paid his bills regularly, without questioning the amounts, and spent a large part of his days in his landlord's company, gaining his confidence, and preparing in other ways for the coup that he had in mind.

"He showed at times considerable sums in notes in his wallet when he was paying his bills, and other signs of having money readily at command, but he didn't flaunt it or boast. He lost a bet for a couple of pounds and paid it cheerfully, treating it lightly, as though the money were nothing to him.

"Then one afternoon he came in after 4:00 P.M. and told some plausible tale about suddenly wanting five hundred pounds which he must have in cash, and could Wall lend it to him till the morning?

"Nicholas Wall is one of those foolish men who think their money is most secure if they keep it under their own eyes and their own keys. He says he had about two thousand pounds in his safe, mostly in bank notes at the time, and he lent the money quite readily—rather proud, I'm inclined to think, that he could show his ability to find such an amount at a moment's notice."

"It sounds very unwise," Mr. Jellipot said, "but you haven't told me the false pretence. I suppose Hamilton represented that he had expectations or means of repayment that don't exist?"

"No. I can't say he did that. He seems to have said very little. He just mentioned that he wanted the money, and let Nicholas Wall push it into his hands. But it was a swindle all right, and must have been planned with knowledge that Wall kept a large sum handy in cash."

"For a hotel proprietor, Mr. Wall appears to have been of an unusually trustful nature."

"Yes. That's how it looks. But he'd been duped in a cunning way, which is where the false pretences come in.

"It began with someone ringing Vincent Hamilton up, and starting conversations in which large investments were proposed in an easy way. The operator—a young fellow who is Wall's nephew—listened in at the switchboard, and became interested.

"In one instance only, there was a message phoned for Hamilton when he was out, which the operator had to take down, advising him to buy Amalgamated Oils heavily for a rise.

"But these phone calls are not evidence against him, particularly unless we can produce the man who sent them, which, so far, we have been unable to do; and as an additional difficulty, for the sake of the reputation of the hotel, Wall is reluctant to make public the fact that Hamilton's telephone conversations were overheard."

"I suppose it frequently happens under such conditions?"

"Yes. Almost normally, you might say. As a fact, the telephone gives an illusion of privacy that doesn't exist. There's always the possibility that an operator will overhear conversations that interest her because she knows the parties concerned, or because she has had her curiosity aroused as to what's going on, and no doubt such knowledge is often abused.

"But in using the public service there is the safeguard that the operators are pledged to secrecy, and most of them value their jobs too much to risk telling anything that might get them into trouble; and, beside that, they're mostly too busy to listen in. There's a measure of safety in the number of conversations they have to handle.

"But a hotel switchboard is a very different proposition. We had a case under investigation a few months ago in which a female operator at a prominent West-End hotel had acquired a small fortune by judicious blackmail based on the information she tapped. She passed it on to a man with whom she was in partnership, and his victims couldn't guess how he obtained the knowledge on which he worked."

"I have no doubt you are right," Mr. Jellipot agreed. "If people were more discreet in their occasions of speech, we lawyers would have comparatively little to do."

"Well, you ought to know best about that; but I should say that my job would be a lot harder than it is now. Nine times out of ten it's because people can't keep their tongues still that we get on the track of the man we want, or the proof we need.... But you can see that it wouldn't do Nicholas Wall any good for him to go into the box to say that he was deceived as to Hamilton's financial position by the fact that he or his staff listened in to conversations that came through on the phone.

"And, beyond that, we couldn't base a charge upon such evidence without setting up that it would be a reasonable presumption on Hamilton's part that the hotel staff would act in that manner. And if Wall had been prepared to do that, you wouldn't get any jury to convict on such grounds.

"No. We had to tell him that he had been done in a way that the law couldn't reach, unless we could obtain some separate evidence to support the charge, and in the endeavour to get that we started tapping Hamilton's telephone conversations ourselves, and I followed him everywhere that he went, and checked up the record of almost everyone that he spoke to for the next fortnight. But I had to own that I'd drawn a blank, and at last we advised Wall to take civil proceedings for anything they may be worth, which will probably not be much."

"You might," the solicitor suggested, "have traced the notes, and seen whether whatever Hamilton did with them was consistent with the excuse on which they were borrowed."

"Why," Inspector Combridge smiled good-humouredly, "we actually thought of that! But we drew a blank again. The notes were banked in Manchester by a bookmaker who said he'd taken them the previous day, for a starting price bet made on the course. The money was said to have been put on a favourite who didn't win.

"We couldn't say that this wasn't consistent with the excuse on which Hamilton borrowed the money, because anyone attending the Manchester races would have had to leave next morning before the hour when the banks open."

"You don't think that that may have been the true explanation, and the money really been lost?"

"No, I don't. I don't think it was ever risked on a bet at all. It was just a plot, very carefully thought out, to get five hundred pounds out of Wall's pocket in a way that the law couldn't reach, and the worst of it is that it seems to have come off successfully."

"At which," Mr. Jellipot observed, "you are naturally somewhat annoyed. But I suppose you will get him another time, if you don't now. The present point is that you are in a position to prove that he could have had no connection with Mr. Hamilton's death, if it were the result of foul play, which is no more than a suspicion as yet, based on the disreputable assertion of an anonymous letter.

"But if a crime should have been committed, such as would shut out the daughter from benefiting under the will, doesn't it suggest that Mr. Wall may get paid after all?"

"You mean that Vincent Hamilton may come into part of the estate?"

"It is at least a possible contingency, in which event you will observe that Nicholas Wall must be included among those who would benefit by the alleged crime."

Mr. Jellipot made this remark in no more than a jesting way and Inspector Combridge took it for the whimsical absurdity that it was, until memory of how the solicitor had once before produced what had seemed to him to be an incredibly improbable murderer entered his mind, and led him to say: "I suppose you're not going to ask me to arrest Wall as the guilty man?"

Mr. Jellipot was a quiet-mannered lawyer, who might smile at times, but from whom open laughter was seldom heard. Now he rejected this fantastic theory with as broad a smile as he was likely to show, but with the precision of statement which was equally characteristic of his legal habitudes.

"No, I don't think I shall ask you to do that. Even if we assume—and it is a large assumption at present—that Mrs. Hamilton has died from other than what are usually described as natural causes, the proposition would still appear to involve that Nicholas Wall must have suborned Ada Hamilton to murder her stepmother (as he could himself have had no direct access to the deceased) with the attractive prospect of being hanged for murder and losing her inheritance, so that it might pass to Vincent Hamilton and become available to discharge his debts, her conviction being a necessary precedent to the culmination at which he aimed.... No, I think a more plausible theory would be required."

"So," Inspector Combridge replied, "it appeared to me." He rose to go as he spoke and, as he did so, an office-boy entered, with a slip of paper, which he handed to Mr. Jellipot, who read it and said: "Yes, I will see her myself. Ask her to wait a moment.... It is Miss Hamilton," he explained as the boy retired. "I suppose I had

17

better hear what she has to say." His thought was that if Vincent Hamilton were a fair specimen, Inspector Combridge had introduced him to a particularly disreputable family, and probably to a case which he would have much preferred not to have in his highly respectable office. But he only added: "Perhaps it will be best for you to go out by the other door."

CHAPTER III.

ADA HAMILTON entered Mr. Jellipot's office. She was a rather tall, blonde girl of about twenty, with large grey eyes which could become innocent and appealing with instant ease on all appropriate occasions, heavily carmined lips, and a complexion which looked as though it might have been good without the artificial assistance which it had certainly had.

"Inspector Combridge," she said, in a pleasantly-modulated, rather nervous voice, "advised me to come and see you."

Mr. Jellipot was a middle-aged bachelor whose associations with women had been for many years almost entirely professional. In that capacity he observed them from many angles, though most usually as the occasions of trouble, and frequently as its active originators also. He was a man of much natural insight, and with a capacity for logical deduction which had enabled him to reach the truth of two baffling crimes when their professional investigators had failed to find it, although the bulk of his practice was not of a criminal character.

Given the necessary data, he would be less likely than a younger man either to fail in judgment of a woman's character, or to be deflected from a considered opinion by any cajolery that she might attempt. But it remained that a younger man, and particularly one leading a less secluded life, might be better able to assess the significances of Miss Hamilton's appearance, and of the war-paint which she had considered appropriate for the present call. As it was, he was conscious of a slight attraction, a faint repulsion, and a more definite distaste for this business which Inspector Combridge had thrust upon him.

He showed, however, nothing of these feelings in the quiet cordiality with which he received his visitor, and guided her to the padded comfort of the low chair which was placed for single clients (or for the most important among several), at the left side of his desk.

"Yes," he said, "I know Inspector Combridge. You must tell me what I can do for you."

Gaining confidence from the cordiality of his voice, and a somewhat deceptive diffidence of manner which was habitual to him, she came to the point with a simple directness which he approved.

"I've come to see you about an anonymous letter that's made a great deal of trouble. I want to find out who wrote it."

"Anonymous letters," he replied, "usually do. They can rarely be justified either ethically or on practical grounds. I have always advised that they should be disregarded in the absence of corroboration of a most definite kind."

"Mr. Lamson didn't take it that way."

"Mr. Lamson being the coroner?"

"Yes. It was about my stepmother's death. It was a wicked letter, as well as a silly one. It suggested that someone had poisoned her."

"And the coroner took it seriously?"

"Yes. He got an order for exhumation. It seems a dreadful thing that someone can make so much trouble without signing his name."

"His?"

"His or hers. I don't know. I wish I did."

Mr. Jellipot, remembering Inspector Combridge's statement that Miss Hamilton had favoured the exhumation, had to remind himself of the danger of forming opinions beyond the logic of the known facts, and that he had accepted her as his client, and must dispose his mind to adopt her interests as his own. But his question was blunt, though it was gently put: "You did not approve the exhumation?"

"Of course not. Who would? But I thought it best to pretend I did. I thought if I seemed unwilling they might suppose there really was something wrong, and be more likely to do it than if I said that I didn't care."

There was a disarming frankness about this explanation, even though it admitted that she could show a different attitude toward those she wished to mislead.

Mr. Jellipot said only: "Probably you were right.... I suppose you are not in any doubt yourself as to the cause of Mrs. Hamilton's death?"

"If you mean do I think anyone poisoned her, not the least. The idea's absurd. As though anyone would! Why, there was no one who went near her except myself, and sometimes one of the maids. And mother and I usually ate the same things, so that cook would have done us both in at the same time, if she'd wanted to. But why should she? Besides, she isn't the sort."

"You were with your stepmother most of the time?"

"Yes. Especially during the last fortnight. She didn't seem really ill, but she wasn't well enough to go out, and Dr. Burfoot came in once or twice, and said he thought someone ought to be with her, in case anything happened suddenly; so, of course, I stayed in."

"Yes. Naturally. So you feel sure that the result of the enquiry will be to show that Mrs. Hamilton died from natural causes?"

"Yes, there's no doubt about that. What I mean to find out is who wrote that beastly letter."

"The adjourned inquest will be on Friday? So I believe it has been announced in the press. You don't think we'd better delay enquiries till after that? Till it's been proved that it was a baseless insinuation?"

"No. I don't see why we should."

"Very well. I'm not sure that I do, either. I suppose you've no idea who may have written it?"

"Not the least. I've tried to imagine who could, but I can't even make a sensible guess."

She said this was an apparent sincerity, but it was not a reply which Mr. Jellipot was disposed to take without further effort.

"I am sure," he said, "that you will realize the importance of giving me all the information and assistance you can, if my services are to be of any benefit to you. Any suggestion, however improbable it may seem—"

"Yes," she answered, "of course I understand that. But I haven't the least idea....

"That," she added, giving him an appealing glance, "is why I have come to you."

"Very well," he said, "if that's really all you can say, I'd better have a look at the letter itself, and see what can be done.... Do you wish me to attend the inquest on your behalf? But probably there's already someone representing the family interests there?"

"I'd much rather you did, if you don't mind."

"Very well. If those are your instructions, I will attend to watch your interests only. You had better let me have your telephone number, in case I want to see you again before then."

He rose as he spoke, and Ada Hamilton took the hint, and rose also. She gave the number he required, shook hands, and went with no more than one appealing, confident glance. He considered, when she had gone, that it was improbable that the writer could be traced

21

before the resumed inquest would be held, and that enquiries might best be made when its results would be known; but it could do no harm to Ada Hamilton for it to appear that she was boldly seeking to discover the authorship in advance of whatever revelation there might be to come. Was that her real object, he wondered? Was he acting for a murderess, as clever as she was wicked, who was making him the catspaw of the attitude of innocence which she had resolved to assume? Who had even got round Inspector Combridge, which he did not think that most criminals found it easy to do?

He did not think that she had the appearance of a woman who would be likely to poison members of her family (even stepmothers, who are traditionally unloved!), but he remembered the inspector's experienced verdict that murderers seldom do.

Well, he was in for it now! And it was his evident duty to consider his client innocent in the absence of conclusive contrary evidence. He had better see the letter—and perhaps have a talk with the coroner's officer—and perhaps a few words with Dr. Burfoot also, if he could think of a sufficient excuse.

Confound Inspector Combridge! He concluded, with unusual violence of thought, why couldn't he leave him alone? He neither wished to defend a murderess, nor to be occupied in investigating a mare's nest, or running the writer of a wickedly mischievous letter to earth, after it had missed fire. He was a conveyancing lawyer, with his hands full of business of more respectable and probably more remunerative descriptions. Why couldn't Combridge leave him alone?

CHAPTER IV.

MR. JELLIPOT telephoned the coroner's office immediately after Ada Hamilton's departure, and received the expected assurance that, as her solicitor, he would be free to inspect the anonymous letter which had originated the enquiry, and beyond that, that Mr. Lamson would be grateful for any assistance he might be able to render in the difficult task of tracing its writer.

He made an appointment for ten-thirty on the following morning, and deferred further consideration of the matter in the meantime to meet the claims of more urgent business.

He called at Mr. Lamson's office at the appointed time, and was received by that gentleman himself with a gratifying cordiality.

The English coroner is usually a member of the medical or legal profession, his duties requiring a combination of the qualifications of these learned specialists, and his attitude toward, and mode of conducting, the investigations he undertakes is inevitably biased by the profession to which he belongs.

Mr. Lamson was a solicitor who had been the practising head of the well-known firm of Lamson & Pendleton before he had nominally rather than actually retired, on undertaking the duties of his present office.

"The fact is, Mr. Jellipot," he said at once, "that it's one of those borderline cases where it might be said that there was no justification for applying for an exhumation order at all, and though I shouldn't like you to misunderstand me to say that I hope there has been any foul play, it's a fact that, unless that should be proved by the medical evidence, it will leave me with a feeling that I've done an almost indefensible thing.

"It's easy to say that, if there be any suspicion raised, however baseless it may be, it's best for the relatives themselves that there should be a proper enquiry, such as will dispose of it effectually; but, on the other hand, it would be a monstrous state of affairs if any malicious scoundrel, or perhaps a mere practical joker, could put respectable people to the annoyance of a post-mortem enquiry of this kind by merely sending me an anonymous letter."

"Then I may conclude that, apart from the letter you mention, there is at present no suspicious circumstance in connection with Mrs. Hamilton's decease?"

"Nothing but that, and a telephone call of the same category— I'll show you our record of that—so that the case depends absolutely upon the nature of the medical analyst's report. And, between ourselves, I never like these murder cases overmuch that are based entirely upon evidence of that kind. We have to take the words of experts on matters we don't understand at all, and they don't only contradict each other, they all talk about scientific facts as though they were of an unchangeable certainty, and we know all the time that they are clever guesses at best, and half the things that we were taught yesterday are denied today."

Mr. Jellipot did not entirely agree. He thought that a case of alleged murder raises two distinct questions. Has a murder been done? And, if so, by whom?

With the second of these questions the medical expert may have no concern; but, in regard to the first, his observations of the effects which poisons produce in the bodies of those they destroy are evidence of a most important, and may be of an essential kind. But his duty to his present client certainly did not require that he should emphasize this orthodox view, so he turned the subject by saying: "I am instructed by Miss Ada Hamilton personally. I suppose that I shall be in order in appearing at the inquest on her behalf? I mean, there must almost certainly be solicitors who have been dealing with the family's financial affairs, and who have already assumed that they are in order in acting in this capacity?"

"Yes, there is such a firm: Ord, Ord, & Shaftsbury, in Carthill Gardens. They have dealt for many years, I am told, with matters connected with the estate. But I don't think they would consider themselves as having any duty to Ada Hamilton personally. Perhaps rather the other way. I believe they were Mrs. Hamilton's solicitors rather than her husband's, and she transferred everything to them when he died. Ada Hamilton would be a mere stepchild to them.... But here comes the letter."

As he spoke, a clerk entered the room, bringing the letter in a glass-covered case, which Mr. Lamson removed with the remark, as he passed it over: "It has been examined for fingerprints with an absolutely negative result."

Mr. Jellipot looked at a piece of rather coarse white writing-paper, on which was printed in clumsy capitals:

MRS. HAMILTON OF 33A GRAFTON TERRACE DIED OF HEART FAILURE, I DON'T THINK! TELL THEM TO LOOK FOR A RARE DRUG. AND DON'T FORGET THAT MOST STEP-MOTHERS ARE BEST OUT OF THE WAY, ES-PECIALLY WHEN THEY'VE GOT EVERY-THING TILL THEY DIE.

Mr. Jellipot turned the paper over in his hand, and found that no inspiration came.

"The writer," he said, "makes his meaning clear. But I am afraid that the discovery of his identity raises questions which are somewhat out of my range. May I ask whether you have any grounds for suspecting who it may be?"

"No. I wish we had. I can tell you this. The paper and envelope are of the same quality, and were probably purchased together. They were manufactured by a Maidstone firm, who make them up into shilling packets of cheap stationery, which they supply to between one and two hundred London customers, and to many others throughout the country. The ink used is Stephens' blue-black. There was a minute grease-spot on the back of the envelope, which the Scotland Yard analyst who has been kind enough to give me his assistance believes to be New Zealand butter.

"You will see that the wording and composition indicate a person of some education, and of sufficient intelligence to avoid the common trick of misspelling the words. The absence of finger-marks suggests that the letter was the result of a deliberate and careful plot.

"The police would be as glad as myself to interview the writer, and ask him a few pointed questions; but they regard it as practically impossible to prove the authorship of such a document, unless the writer does something foolish by which he gives himself away."

"Whoever wrote it," Mr. Jellipot suggested, "must have been acquainted with the family affairs, and with the provisions of Mr. Hamilton's will. He or she suggests a knowledge of the drug with which the alleged murder was committed. It appears that such knowledge could be possessed by few, and the area of enquiry must be correspondingly narrow."

"So it does," Mr. Lamson agreed, "though the number of such persons is larger than you might suppose at a first guess, and unfortunately includes no one to whom a particular suspicion can be attached.

"Inspector Combridge—a most efficient man in my judgment, though his reputation needs no endorsement by me—made a list of over fifty people to whom those conditions might possibly apply, which subsequent scrutiny reduced to about half the number, which is not certainly complete, as it is evident that anyone might be in Ada Hamilton's confidence sufficiently to become suspicious, of whom we may have obtained no knowledge at all."

"But not many who would have any financial interest in the matter?

"No. But can we conclude certainly that the writer must be found within that category? Might he or she not be impelled by an abstract desire to promote the interests of justice, if something had been indiscreetly confided, or overseen or heard, which indicated the crime?"

Mr. Jellipot accepted this theoretic possibility in a somewhat absentminded manner. He was more interested in the revelation of the extent to which Inspector Combridge had been investigating the origin of the letter himself before recommending Miss Hamilton to engage him upon the same quest. He felt, with a mild resentment, that it was unreasonable to ask him to undertake such a matter, in which those who specialized in detective work were admittedly on a cold scent. Still, it was open to him to instruct a private agency to undertake that which was outside the range of his own office, and certainly beyond his own inclination, if not his dignity, to pursue personally. Probably Combridge had expected him to do this, while appearing for Ada Hamilton at the inquest, and using the information he might obtain as her interests might require.

These reflections, instantly made, led him, by an apparent process, to ask: "I suppose Vincent Hamilton's on the list?"

Mr. Lamson smiled slightly. "Yes. He certainly is! I expect Inspector Combridge told you about him. He put him first, and, if he'd known how to do it, he'd have ended where he began.

"But there's really nothing to identify the letter with him more than a dozen others, probably more. And, if you give it a moment's thought, you'll see that the fact that we may be able to say that this letter was written by one of two or three dozen people doesn't help us as much as anyone might suppose.

"Whoever wrote it must be prepared for the possibility of being questioned, and isn't likely to admit it. He can't be taken by surprise. He'll probably deny it just as convincingly as the others will do who are quite innocent. And when you've questioned them all, what have you done beyond putting the writer more on his guard than he was before?

"No, I should say it's the better plan to be quiet till you've got something better to go on, or until the writer does something further that helps to give him away."

"You said there was a telephone message, following this letter?"

"So I did. I'm coming to that. I ought to explain to you that when I got the letter I didn't act instantly. At least, not in any way that could be publicly known.

"I wasn't at all sure that it deserved anything better than the hottest part or the fire, but I sent my assistant to interview Dr. Burfoot confidentially, and to ask him if he had given his certificate of death without hesitation, or whether there had been any element of doubt, or suspicious symptoms which had come under his notice.

"Dr. Burfoot acted as it might be expected he would. He came round to see me himself, and was extremely frank in the statement he made.

"He said that, rightly or wrongly, the idea of foul play had never entered his mind. He had thought the cause of death to be simple and obvious in the case of an elderly patient who had been troubled with valvular weakness for several years, and whom he had seen two days previously.

"He said that when he saw her then she had been in worse health than a fortnight before, and though he was rather surprised to be called in hurriedly two days later, and to find her dead when he arrived, there was nothing abnormal or improbable in such an event, and after he had heard Miss Ada's account of what had occurred, he gave the certificate without hesitation crossing his mind.

"He said that he was still of opinion that Mrs. Hamilton had died in a natural way, and from the causes which his certificate set out; but as to denying the *possibility* that death might have been caused or hastened by the administration of some poisonous drug—well, it was more than he, or any other doctor, without a post-mortem, could do.

"If I asked his opinion, it was still that she had died a natural death, and it was an opinion which it would take more than an anonymous letter to shake. He based that opinion both on his medical knowledge, and his observation of the people concerned.

"But if I asked him for a professional *assurance* that the death had been correctly set out on the certificate, he was bound to reply that he could not give it, and that it was a question that nothing short of a post-mortem examination would answer with final certainty."

"The certificate of death," Mr. Jellipot remarked, "seems to have been rather carelessly given. Perhaps it would not be going beyond the facts to conclude that they often are?"

"Yes. That is commonly true, though every doctor would not be as frank as Dr. Burfoot in such admission. Indeed, what else can you expect? In an enormous majority of cases the remotest suspicion does not arise, and yet, in a very large proportion of such deaths, it would be impossible, without a post-mortem, to rule out the remote contingency that some form or degree of poisoning—some deliberate hastening of death—may have occurred.

"But what practice would a doctor be likely to keep if it became known that he had a disposition to bring to my notice the fact that poison could not be absolutely ruled out as a possibility when his patients died?

"Actually, there are few doctors within my district in whom I should have as much confidence as in Dr. Burfoot to detect anything of an illicit kind, should it actually occur."

"So that, I suppose," Mr. Jellipot concluded, "Dr. Burfoot's statement left you very much where you were before?"

"Yes, except that he himself suggested that, with my permission, he should mention the anonymous letter to Ada Hamilton, and ask her whether she could suggest anything as to its origin, and also whether she would be disposed to raise any objection if I should consider an exhumation desirable.

"He did this, and reported to me two days later that Miss Hamilton, while showing some natural indignation, and professing incredulity, had said that, if the allegation were taken seriously, whatever investigation might be considered necessary would have her consent. And the same morning I was rung up here, presumably by the writer of the anonymous letter, who may have feared that his first shot had missed fire, as the days passed, and he could observe nothing occur.

"A call came through from a 'Mr. Nimmo,' who said that he wished to speak to me personally on a matter he could not discuss with others. The clerk who took the call had the wit to think there was something queer about the name and the manner of the request, and had a word with me before putting me through, as a result of which I told him to listen in, and if he thought there was a cause, to get the telephone operator on another line and ask them to check up the number from which the call came.

"One result of this was that both Pierce and I heard the first message, which was all that mattered—after that I was merely occupied in trying to prolong the conversation so that the speaker might be caught, if possible, and we agreed the words immediately afterwards, and I had them written down. This is what they were: 'I just thought I should like to know what you're doing about the Hamilton murder case. You've had time enough to split it wide open now, if you know your job.'

"I replied that if I were speaking to the writer of an anonymous letter which I had received during the previous week, I could only tell him that a properly signed statement would have immediate attention.

"To which he replied, as nearly as we could recall it: 'So that's it, is it? A signed statement? No, I don't think I will. There's a law of libel, you know; and, after all, it's your duty, not mine. I think I've done enough in giving you the straight tip.'

"After that, I suggested that, if he were afraid to make a signed statement, perhaps he wouldn't mind calling here, and giving what information he could, which would be treated confidentially, at least unless, or until, it should be substantiated by our own investigations.

"I didn't suppose he would come. I was just trying to hold him to the phone as long as possible. But he only said: 'Not for yours truly. If you won't act, you'll find I'll make it public another way,' and then rang off before I had time to reply."

"You didn't trace him, of course?"

"No. It appeared that he was speaking from one of the callboxes in the Underground station at Piccadilly Circus. You can judge what chance there would be that anyone would notice him there.

"I dare say it wasn't thirty seconds before Scotland Yard was informed, and probably not half a minute longer before the station police were at the box, but a young woman had just entered it who had nothing to do with the matter. She said she had seen no one come out. It had been vacant as she approached. In fact, no one could be found who had observed anything of the previous occupant of the box."

"It appears," Mr. Jellipot remarked, "to help us so far that it eliminates any woman suspects, if I infer correctly from what you say that you are clear that it was a man who spoke; and there is the possibility that you might recognize the voice, if you should hear it again."

"Yes. Perhaps I might. But I can't say that it would be easy to do. My impression was that it was intentionally indistinct, and disguised by a nasal intonation."

"A nasal voice," Mr. Jellipot commented, "is naturally suggestive of an American origin. Isn't 'split it wide open' an American idiom?"

"Yes. Familiar to everyone who attends the cinemas. There's no reliance on that."

Mr. Jellipot felt that he had learnt all he could from this source, and more than most coroners might have been willing to tell.

With a few words of appropriate thanks, and a remark that he would be at the inquest on Friday, he got up to go.

CHAPTER V.

MR. JELLIPOT returned to his office in some uncertainty of decision as to whether he should do anything further in the matter until after the adjourned inquest had been held.

The investigation which had been thrust upon him was not one which he was disposed to continue personally. He considered that his time was too valuable, and his dignity was not free from hazard.

He was at this time the head of a large and busy office, his practice having rapidly grown since his acquaintance with Sir Reginald Crowe, the chairman of the London and Northern Bank, had led to a considerable proportion of the legal business which the bank controlled being placed in his hands. He did not expect to call upon clients: they came to him.

He saw that this enquiry was of a nature to be undertaken by a private detective agency, who would probably handle it far more efficiently than he would himself.

But he hesitated to call in such a firm a mere twenty-four hours before the inquest would be held, and the result of the post-mortem known.

Tomorrow, his client would either be under grave suspicion, if not actual accusation of murder, or the writer of the anonymous letter would be shown to have circulated a scandalous and malicious lie.

In the latter case, the writer would probably be liable both for civil damages and to criminal prosecution. In the former, he might have little to fear from any legal process, and to discover him might even be to provide an additional, and perhaps deadly, witness for the prosecution of Ada Hamilton.

Every instinct of legal caution urged him to wait, but he did not forget that his instructions were of an opposite purpose. Ada Hamilton had said that she wished the enquiry to be pressed forward at once, putting the question of murder aside as a fantastic improbability. What right had he to delay, or deviate from, those instructions

31

on an assumption that his client might be guilty of the alleged crime?

From another angle, he felt that he would be glad to know definitely, before he should go into court tomorrow, what was the nature of the case with which he would have to deal, and both considerations led him to consider whether there were no means by which he could learn the result of the autopsy that afternoon.

There were two people who could probably tell him—Dr. Burfoot and Sir Lionel Tipshift, who had conducted the post-mortem on behalf of the Crown. No doubt, when the result were known, the coroner also would be promptly informed.

But in the case of Sir Lionel Tipshift it was improbable that direct enquiry would be met by anything better than a blank refusal, and with both him and the coroner an enquiry was open to the objection that it was not in Miss Hamilton's interest that he should appear to be anxious, as though anticipating an incriminating result.

Dr. Burfoot remained. Here also a direct enquiry in advance of the inquest might be rebuffed, but why not seek an interview with him as soliciting his aid in the discovery of the anonymous letter-writer? If he could engage the doctor in such conversation, he thought it improbable that he could avoid, by implication if not by explicit statement, revealing that which the post-mortem had shown.

The result of these reflections was that he rang up Dr. Burfoot's address during the afternoon, and was not sorry to learn that he was out. He was expected back before six. Would he be free after that? His surgery hours were from 7:00 to 8:00 P.M. Very well, please tell him, when he should come in, that Mr. Jellipot would call upon him at 6:30 P.M. That should give him leisure for a meal, and yet with no opportunity to cancel the appointment, for Mr. Jellipot would have left his office before the time at which he was expected to return from his afternoon round.

As he journeyed to the doctor's residence on a bus top (for though of ample means, and capable of substantial generosities, he was of habitual frugality in his personal expenditure). Mr. Jellipot faced the question of what his future course of action should be if it should appear that Mrs. Hamilton had died by a poisoner's hands.

In that event, he was already sufficiently familiar with the facts to see that Ada Hamilton was probably, if not certainly guilty of murder in one of its basest forms, and his inclination would be to retire from the case. He was not normally a criminal lawyer, and Inspector Combridge should have known him too well to thrust such business upon him. Yet he felt that justice would require that he should not take that course unless he were satisfied that there was no reasonable doubt of the guilt of this unwelcome client, and for that question to be resolved it might become necessary to examine exhaustively all methods by which the fatal substance could have been accidentally or deliberately taken, or administered by someone, other than Ada, who would have had the necessary access to the invalid.

Among these last he observed that Dr. Burfoot must be included, and though he did not regard it as a reasonable supposition that a medical practitioner of whom the coroner had spoken favourably should have poisoned a remunerative patient, with nothing apparent to be gained by her death, yet he was led to consider, as an abstract question, how easily a doctor could increase the mortality among those he attended, if he were of a disposition to do so, either from experimental or sadistic motives, with the comfortable knowledge that his own signature would be accepted as sufficient assurance that they had not been hastened to death....

Dr. Burfoot, a tall, spare man whose sixty-five years had not reduced the alert activities either of mind or body, received him with courtesy, and with no lack of frankness when he learnt the business on which he came.

"I have no doubt," he said, "that as solicitor to Miss Hamilton—or indeed, to any member of the family of the deceased—you are entitled to all the information that I can give you. And," he added with gravity, "I wish it were of an opposite kind to what it is.

"I consider that I was invited to be present at the autopsy as representing Mrs. Hamilton's family, as well as being the one who had signed the death certificate which was anonymously challenged, and which, I am sorry to say, in the light of our present knowledge, was inadequate, if not precisely incorrect.

"My own position is of minor importance, but on that point Sir Lionel Tipshift was generous enough to say that he would himself have given the same certificate under similar circumstances.

"I certified Mrs. Hamilton's death as being due to cardiac failure, as in fact it was. I attributed that condition to a diseased valvular condition for which I had attended her for several years, and as recently as the fortnight before she died. It was a natural deduction, but, as we now know, it was wrong.

"I must tell you that I had not the faintest suspicion of foul play at the time, and even now I find it difficult to believe.

"Up to a point, the post-mortem confirmed my own certification. There was no doubt that heart failure was the primary cause of death.

"It is also established beyond doubt that the organs were free from any of the familiar poisons, such as are most often used either criminally or for self-destruction, and to that extent I am absolved from having overlooked symptoms such as a medical man should be alert to observe.

"But Sir Lionel, who, in such matters, has a far wider experience than my own, was intrigued by certain conditions of the aorta, into the technical details of which I need not enter, but which I will own (between ourselves) that I should not have regarded as sufficiently abnormal to arouse suspicion."

"Perhaps," Mr. Jellipot suggested mildly, "that may have been because they were actually innocent?"

"I am afraid not. Sir Lionel observed that these conditions were at least consistent with those which occur as the result of the injection of a certain drug which has only become very recently known, and which is now being used in dentistry as a local anæsthetic.

"I do not mean to imply that it can have any fatal, or even detrimental effect upon the heart when used in the local manner that dental surgery requires; but it appears that there have been extensive vivisectional experiments carried out recently upon various animals, including a number of dogs, of which Sir Lionel Tipshift has been cognizant, to ascertain whether it could be safely used in larger quantities, and for major operations. The result of this has been the disconcerting discovery that it is likely to act upon the motor nerves in a peculiar manner, causing paralysis of various muscles, including that of the heart, and Sir Lionel thought that he observed indications similar to those which he had seen in the hearts of animals who had died from that cause.

"It therefore became necessary to have a further analysis directed to the detection of this drug, for which no previous test had been made, and I regret to say that the result is to justify Sir Lionel's suspicions, and to make it a scientific certainty that Mrs. Hamilton received a fatal dosage, either in her food or by intravenous injection, within a few hours of her death."

"If," Mr. Jellipot observed, "it should be regarded as an admitted fact that Mrs. Hamilton died from this obscure form of poisoning, we should still, I suggest, be a very long way from concluding that it had been deliberately administered, either with or without criminal intention, and still further from identifying any individual with such an action."

Dr. Burfoot did not assent. He became silent, and when at last he spoke his voice had an increased gravity: "You will understand, of course, that I am neither making nor suggesting anything against

Miss Hamilton. I am simply telling you what the police are certain to discover, and of which, therefore, you, as her solicitor, should be equally informed. But it is a fact that, until a few weeks ago, Miss Hamilton was employed as secretary-receptionist by a firm of dentists in Corbin Street—at the moment, I do not recall the name."

"Where she would have had access to this drug?"

"I cannot answer that. Most probably, yes."

"Can you say why she left?"

"I believe it was because her stepmother felt increasingly unfit to be left alone."

Mr. Jellipot saw some support in that statement for argument that Mrs. Hamilton had died from a natural cause. Weeks before, she had been conscious of failing health, and unwilling to be left. In that condition, she had looked to her stepdaughter for help, and the sacrifice of her own career, showing confidence, and probably affection, which seemed to have been reciprocated, or why had Ada consented to give up the salary, and with it the measure of independence, she had? In the absence of anything more than a vague suspicion being directed against her, a clever counsel could surely make something of that!

But his next thought was that it could be as easily used in a directly opposite way. The stepmother, who had been hated before, became an intolerable nuisance when she required that Ada should give her whole time to waiting upon her sick and elderly whims. And so the evil thought comes to her stepdaughter's mind that she can be removed in this easy, unguessable manner, being the invalid she already is, and no longer control the wealth, and consume the time, which those who are still young can put to better uses than she.

"You have known the family a good many years, Dr. Burfoot?" he asked.

"Yes. Almost all my professional life."

"I am in a different position. I have only been consulted during the last twenty-four hours, and Ada Hamilton is a stranger to me. I will tell you frankly that it is a case I do not like.

"I have never felt a disposition to specialize in criminal business, although I have been professionally concerned by a combination of circumstances in one or two notorious cases, and nothing would incline me to give my time to working up the defence of a suspected poisoner, except a conviction that I were acting for a person innocently accused. Will you be good enough to tell me—of course in the strictest confidence—whether it is a case in which you think I should be further concerned?"

Dr. Burfoot did not refuse to reply, but he did not appear to find the question easy to answer. He sat with his legs crossed, and a foot moving restlessly, on which his eyes fell, and Mr. Jellipot was content to wait for him to speak at his own time.

He said at last: "You ask me a very difficult question, but I think the right reply is that I am aware of no suspicious or detrimental circumstance other than that of which you are already informed.

"Beside that, there is the question of the anonymous letter. It seems to me that if you could discover its writer, and the circumstances which caused it to be written, you could judge the facts of the case much better than you can now."

Mr. Jellipot approved the discretion of this reply, which reminded him that he had intended to make that letter an excuse for his call, which he had found it needless to use. He now asked, in a more genuine mood: "I suppose you are not able to help me with any suggestion as to who it might be?"

"No, I can't say that I am. If we—if anyone—were to assume that Ada Hamilton procured the drug from the stock of the dentists by whom she was employed, it might be worth while to look for the writer of the letter in the same direction. But that's a mere guess, and you might think it to be the kind that anyone who is defending her innocence ought not to make."

"Miss Hamilton's instructions to me," Mr. Jellipot replied, "were to find the writer of the letter, by any possible means. She professed this to be her first anxiety, putting aside the idea that her stepmother had really been poisoned as something too fantastic to entertain."

"That is a very natural attitude if she be innocent, as I should like to believe."

"And otherwise," Mr. Jellipot reflected aloud, "the discovery might be of less than no assistance to her."

Dr. Burfoot did not dissent from this conclusion, and Mr. Jellipot, with a remark that they would meet again in the morning, got up to go.

His mind had clarified itself since the question of the letter had been discussed.

Ada Hamilton had instructed him to discover its origin, without consideration of consequences. If she were not guilty, it was the wisest thing she could do. If he accepted her protestation of innocence, and carried out her instructions successfully, there could be no blame to himself, even though she had lied to him and the result should be to ensure her condemnation.

He decided to concentrate upon this investigation, and not, in the absence of unexpected developments, to abandon the case before he had run the writer to earth; after which he would act according to the circumstances as he would then judge them to be.

CHAPTER VI.

IT was obvious that the course on which Mr. Jellipot had resolved must involve his appearance as Miss Hamilton's solicitor at
the coroner's court, for the inquest was to be held at 10:30 A.M. on
Friday, and it was Thursday evening when he parted from Dr. Burfoot. It was too late to return to his office, and as he sat in the Wimbledon train on his way home to a dinner which must be held back
somewhat later than his usual hour, he realized that he could do little
more toward tracing the authorship of the letter until after tomorrow's enquiry; and though he might feel that he had been drawn into
a case from which he would be glad to retire, his sense of professional honour would not therefore permit him to fail his client, be
she poisoner or what else she might, so long as he should continue
to represent her.

He considered later, as he surrendered to his solitary bachelor
vice of an after-dinner cigar, that it was due to her that she should be
informed of the result of the post-mortem before going into court
tomorrow, and that a conference with her would be desirable.

He had her address, and there would still be time for him to
write, asking her to call upon him at 9:30 A.M. tomorrow. But he
also had her telephone number, which supplied a speedier and less
troublesome method of communication. Remembering this, he decided to ring her up.

He got through at once, and heard her voice in reply.

"Oh, yes, Mr. Jellipot, it's I speaking. Have you found anything
out?" There was a note of excitement in the words, as though of a
pleased anticipation of what she would be likely to hear.

"No. Not about the matter on which you primarily consulted
me. I have made some enquiries, but so far with no more than negative results, which is, perhaps, all that you could reasonably anticipate in so short a time. But I have received information in reference
to the enquiry tomorrow which makes it desirable that I should see
you beforehand."

"You mean you've not found out anything about that beastly letter, but you want to see me before the inquest about something else?"

Her voice sounded flat and disappointed, as though anything else must be subordinate in importance to that which she had asked him to do. Was she acting, he wondered, or was she really oblivious of the potential seriousness of her own position? He felt that her attitude made it more important that he should talk plainly to her, and his professional caution was disturbed by the bluntness of her reply to the careful vagueness of his own allusions.

"Yes," he said. "It is necessary for me to see you. I am speaking from Wimbledon, where I live. Perhaps it would be possible for you to come over to see me tonight? A taxi would do it in half an hour."

"I don't know," she said.

"Perhaps I could." There was indecision, even unwillingness in the voice. "The fact is," she added, "I was just going out when you rang up."

Her casual treatment of the matter increased the urgency of the occasion to his mind.

"Unless," he said, "it is a matter of very great importance, I think it might be wiser to put it aside. I could discuss the matter at more leisure than may be possible in the morning."

"I can't say it's exactly that. I was going out with a friend. Can't you tell me now what it is you want me to know?"

"I'm afraid not. The telephone is not, for several reasons, a desirable medium of communication."

"Oh, well. If it's really something you can't say on the phone!" There was a mingling of exasperation and resignation in her voice as she added: "I suppose I'd better come now. What a curse the whole thing is!"

He gave her his address, to which she answered: "Yes, I've got that down. I'll come at once. It's very good of you to be troubling about it at this time of night."

He was mollified by this somewhat belated recognition of his efforts on her behalf, though no nearer to a decision as to whether he was about to receive a criminal of a particularly objectionable kind, or an innocent girl who was still without adequate consciousness of the peril in which she stood. With whom, he wondered, had she been intending to spend the evening? If he should ask her that, would her reply give him the name he sought? Certainly, if so, she could not suspect the truth. But was it not the admitted position that neither she nor others were yet able to guess that name? And who more likely than one she regarded as a friend, and with whom she went out at night? Who probably had access to the house, with opportunities to observe what occurred, and to whom her confidences might be given? Yet was not this supposition coming near to assume that she was the murderess that Dr. Burfoot's information had appeared to indicate? And, if the facts were faced, was not that almost certainly what she was?

Well, he would assume nothing. He would wait to hear what she had to say. The position of a suspected and possibly innocent girl was hard indeed if her own solicitor were not prepared to hear her case with an open and friendly mind.

So he told himself as he reviewed the position until, in a rather shorter time than he had expected, her taxi was at the door.

CHAPTER VII.

IT may be a measure of the degree of the reluctant suspicion with which Mr. Jellipot regarded his unsought client that he was conscious of being unexpectedly reassured, even relieved, by her words and manner as she appeared at this second interview.

Afterward, suspicion and doubt might return, as in fact they did, but it remained, and is fair to observe, that the dubiety of the mental conception which he had been forming of her during the day was relieved and diminished, for the moment at least, by this second personal contact.

"I hope," she said, "I didn't sound too ungrateful when I tried to get out of coming. I'm awfully grateful really for all the trouble you're taking. I know solicitors don't reckon to see people like this after office hours. But the fact was that I'd promised to go out with a friend, and I hated putting him off at the last minute. And, beside that, we were going to a picture I particularly wanted to see."

"I am sorry," he said, "to have caused you to break your appointment, but the fact is that I saw Dr. Burfoot this afternoon, and he told me something I thought that you ought to know."

She said nothing to that, and though he saw that the words gained her attention, her manner was not that of one whose liberty, even life itself, might hang on the next words she should hear. But it is notorious that women at such junctures as this can act better than men, appearing to be their superiors (if that be the word), both in duplicity and self-control.

"You are already aware," he went on, feeling that that which he had to tell should not be abruptly approached, and commencing, as it were, some distance away, "that the inquest, after a merely formal opening, was adjourned to allow time for Sir Lionel Tipshift, who usually acts for the Home Office in these matters, to conduct a post-mortem examination, at which Dr. Burfoot was invited to be present, which was due to him, as well as being in your own interest, because he had given the death certificate which was challenged by the anonymous letter.

"I am sorry to say that the result of the post-mortem is to suggest that Mrs. Hamilton did not die from what is generally known as natural causes."

Miss Hamilton looked somewhat troubled, but more decidedly puzzled, by this information. She said: "I don't quite know what you mean."

"I might have been plainer. Sir Lionel Tipshift's opinion is that death resulted from the administration of a poisonous drug."

"I don't believe anything of the kind! He wouldn't have found that unless he'd been told to look for it before he began."

"I don't think that we can dismiss it quite as lightly as that. I understand it to be a conclusion which Dr. Burfoot does not dispute."

"Dr. Burfoot! I should have thought he would have had more sense."

"You mean that you would still wish me to contend that your stepmother died from natural causes, even against the medical evidence with which we shall now be confronted?"

"I'm quite sure she did, if you mean that. But if they've made up their minds to say something different, I don't think we need bother so much. I don't suppose they'd alter if we talked to them all day.... But what I mean is that they wouldn't have found anything of the kind if they hadn't been told what they were to look for before they began.... It's the man who wrote that letter we ought to find, if we want to clear the thing up."

"I am inclined to agree with you about that. But I want you to understand first the position which we shall have to face tomorrow. Sir Lionel's evidence, as I am told, will suggest that Mrs. Hamilton died as a result of taking one or more doses of an obscure drug, which has only recently been discovered, and which is used as a local anaesthetic for tooth extractions."

"But it sounds absurd! She hadn't been near a dentist for years. Not as far as I know, and I think I should."

"Dr. Burfoot told me that you held a secretarial appointment until recently with a firm of dentists."

"But what—?" She stopped abruptly, and her face whitened beneath the cosmetics which were less conspicuous now than they had been in the clearer daylight. "You don't mean that they will say that I had anything to do with getting it for her?"

"It is improbable that any suggestion will be made without evidence in its support. What I am asking now is that you will give me all the facts you can, so that I shall not be unprepared to deal with whatever I may have to meet."

"But—I don't see how I can guess that. I don't know what you want me to say, except that it's all lies, as I'm sure it is."

"Do you mind if I ask you a few questions?"

"No, of course not. I'll tell you anything that I can."

"That will be the best help you can give me, if you will do it without reserve. You may be invited to give evidence tomorrow, though you will be under no obligation to do so, and if it have no other advantage it may clarify your own mind as to the circumstances concerning which you may be asked.... You were, until lately, in the employment of a firm of dentists?"

"Yes—Lobbs & Rider in Corbin Street."

"What were your duties there?"

"I used to receive the patients, and deal with the correspondence, and keep the books, and make out the accounts."

"You did not act as nurse or assistant in the dentistry itself in any capacity?"

"Oh, no. I wasn't trained for that kind of work. I shouldn't have liked it at all."

"Had you anything to do with the administration of anæsthetics?"

"Nothing at all."

"You had access to them?"

"I—I don't know. I never thought about it. I suppose I had."

"How and when?"

"It would depend upon where they were kept. I never thought about it. I used to stay sometimes after the others had left, if there were letters to get off."

Mr. Jellipot paused upon this. It was his own business to accept his client's statements in the absence of contradictory evidence, but she might have to tell her tale to those who would receive it in an opposite spirit. The duties she had described did not seem very onerous, nor likely to require that she would be detained after others had left.

"I am not conversant," he said, "with the details of the organization of the staff of a dental surgery, but the duties you have described struck me as being unusually restricted. Is it a large firm?"

"There's Mr. Lobbs. Mr. Rider's dead. There's Phil—Mr. North, who came into the firm last year. And there's Mr. Riddlestone. They divide the patients between them. Then there's the anæsthetist, Dr. Addison. And there are two workmen on the top floor. And there were Nurse Proctor and I."

43

"I see. Quite a large establishment. And you were fully occupied with the duties of which you have told me?"

"Yes. More or less. I don't say I was overworked. There were times when I was busy, and others when I was slack."

"You have said that you had nothing to do with the anæsthetics. But you would hear talk about the work that went on? You would know more or less what was being done?"

"Not to understand. I know that Dr. Addison was always trying everything new, and Mr. Lobbs didn't approve."

"Dr. Addison is a regular member of the firm?"

"Not exactly. He was paid so much for each case at which he assisted. I know that, because I had to make up his accounts, and he was always bothering about them. He was usually hard up, and wanting to draw money before it was due."

"Tell me this, and please be careful to be exact. Did you ever, under whatever circumstances, have occasion to take home any drug or chemical from the surgery, and, if so, was it left where Mrs. Hamilton might have got to it accidentally or by design?"

"No, I'm quite certain I never did."

"Did anyone else connected with the firm ever visit your home?"

"Mr. North has been."

"And met Mrs. Hamilton?"

"Oh, yes."

"So that you cannot say that he may not have brought such a drug into the house?"

"It doesn't sound likely, does it?"

"No. But we may be dealing with unlikely events. You can't say that he didn't?"

"He isn't the sort to do anything silly."

Mr. Jellipot had an inspiration. "It was he with whom you would have been going out tonight?"

"Yes."

"You are good friends?"

"Yes. Quite."

"More than friends, may I ask?"

"We're engaged, if you mean that."

"Why exactly did you resign your position?"

"I haven't exactly resigned. I stayed away because my stepmother wasn't fit to be left, and they were kind enough to get someone temporary. I'm expecting to go back on Monday week."

"I want you to consider for a moment the matter of the anonymous letter. If we take it as a fact that Mrs. Hamilton died through the action of a certain drug, as I have little doubt that she did, and if it prove to be the case, as it almost certainly will, that that drug is in the possession of Lobbs & Rider, it will be an inevitable consequence that enquiry will be directed to connect these two circumstances. And as you say that you were not the medium by which it was conveyed, any possible alternative will be probed, and in the interests of justice—of your own interests, if you will allow me to say so—it is essential that such scrutiny should be made.

"Now in that connection it appears that whoever wrote that letter must have had some knowledge of, or some means of making a correct guess at the cause of Mrs. Hamilton's death, and that appears to make it probable, though not certain, that it was written by someone on the Corbin Street premises, or connected therewith."

"I don't quite see that, but I've always said that if we could find out who wrote the letter the whole thing would be cleared up. And I feel sure you'll find some way of getting him caught."

As she said this, Miss Hamilton raised her eyes to Mr. Jellipot's face with a pathetic and yet confident appeal to which he was not insensible. She had become increasingly nervous and perturbed in manner as the conversation proceeded, but whether this was because she had gradually come to realize the seriousness of her own position, or that, as the conversation lengthened, she had failed to maintain a mask which had at first been deliberately assumed, Mr. Jellipot was still in doubt when he reviewed the interview through the hours of an unusually wakeful night.

He said now: "You can trust me to do my best. I can't promise success. You tell me that Mr. North is the only one connected with the firm who ever came to your home?"

"He didn't write the letter, if you mean that. The idea's simply absurd."

"Probably so. But if you wish me to clear you from—I should say to clear up the whole matter, you must be content for me to examine every possibility without exception.... Shall you wish to give evidence tomorrow, if you should be asked?"

"I don't see why I shouldn't. There isn't much I could say."

"Neither, at present, do I. And if there is no reason why you shouldn't, there remains a strong reason why you should. But you must leave me to decide that at the time. It is enough for the moment that you will not be unwilling to do so.

"But let me give you one final word of advice. If you go into the witness-box, answer every question accurately; and if you don't understand why it is asked be all the more careful to be exact and explicit in your reply. But don't go beyond the replies to say other things, unless I myself invite you to do so.

"And unless you are asked directly, in which case you should tell the truth, it will be needless to mention Dr. Addison's impecuniosity, or the fact that, when you left Lobbs & Rider, you had any expectation of going back."

With these words, and after offering some refreshment, which she declined, Mr. Jellipot let his visitor go.

He was in a vague way rather better impressed by her personality than he had been at the earlier interview, though he was still in an active doubt.

But, whatever might be the truth, he saw that, by her own account, the case against her was likely to be even stronger than he had feared.

Dr. Addison was chronically short of money, sponging upon the firm, and it was she who made out the statements against which his cheques were issued! And it was he who would be in primary control of the poison by which her stepmother died.

Mr. North was on a footing of friendly intimacy. He came to the house at times. What were the relations, what the understanding, between the two? Her stepmother's death would give her freedom— and wealth which they might be planning to share!

Then she had not left her position. A temporary assistant had been installed. Was not this coming very near to anticipating the event which would leave her free to return? Capable of innocent construction, perhaps; but how damaging it could be made in a clever advocate's mouth!

The point most in her favour was the seemingly unconscious frankness with which she told him of these disconcerting circumstances. Was it the simplicity of innocence, or the cleverness of a woman who saw the necessity of winning him to her side, and was frank about matters which she was shrewd enough to see it would be less dangerous to admit than deny?

Well, it came back to the question of the writer of the letter from which all this had begun. Discover that, and it would be a different problem, and one which should be simpler to solve.

But first, there would be the inquest with which to deal.

CHAPTER VIII.

INSPECTOR COMBRIDGE entered the coroner's court feeling rather uncomfortable. He had known Mr. Jellipot both as colleague and opponent, and learnt to respect him in both capacities, and, beyond that, a cordiality of friendship had developed from these associations which he would not willingly lose.

He was conscious of a complication of motives in introducing Ada Hamilton, for one of which at least Mr. Jellipot could not be expected to thank him.

There had been a quite genuine doubt as to her guilt or innocence, and a willingness to recommend her to a lawyer who, in spite of a hesitant and somewhat diffident manner, and a habit of protesting (with some truth) that he had a very limited experience in the criminal courts, had proved on more than one occasion that he had qualities of insight and tenacity which had brought a storm-beaten bark to unexpected harbour.

Then there had been a less defensible willingness to present the lawyer with what appeared to be the insoluble problem of the anonymous letter. Let Jellipot try his hand at real detective work himself, and he would be able to admire with a finer discrimination the difficult, thankless art that was so much less spectacular than a law-court triumph—which would often appear as simple after its solution as it had looked baffling before. He knew that in his heart he had not really expected him to succeed.

But he would not have directed Miss Hamilton to Mr. Jellipot's office had he known, or even expected, the nature of Sir Lionel Tipshift's report, which had reached his office a few hours later.

He knew that Mr. Jellipot did not ordinarily seek, or accept criminal business. He knew that it must divert his mind from work of a far more remunerative character. He knew that it was personal friendship for himself which had weighed down a doubtful scale, and that, apart from that, Mr. Jellipot would have replied at once that the matter was not one for which he had inclination or time.

Looked at in that way, he felt that he had done rather a caddish thing, which even the apology which he was prepared to make could not adequately adjust.

He met Mr. Jellipot in the outer corridor. "I am afraid," he said, "I brought you a bad egg for breakfast yesterday. If I'd really thought—"

Mr. Jellipot understood him very well, and though he had no intention of making it a cause of quarrel, he was still less inclined to accept condolences, or to enter into conversation based on the assumption that his client was a guilty woman.

He would have liked to reply that Miss Hamilton was a very charming young lady, and a client whom he was honoured to have, but his habitual caution, and a timely memory of the proverb that he laughs longest who laughs last, caused him to leave the words unsaid. "I am sure you did not expect it," he replied pleasantly, "or you would not have recommended Miss Hamilton to me. But, if I may venture an opinion upon a case which I have not yet had sufficient time to study with the care it requires, I should say that there may be surprises for all of us."

He left Inspector Combridge vaguely uncomfortable, and went in to the court in a more combative mood than he had been feeling a moment before.

He sat down with Ada Hamilton immediately behind him, and an elderly lawyer with a parchment-like, many-wrinkled face, whom he recognized as Dudley Ord, at his side.

"I have been instructed," he said to him, "by Miss Ada Hamilton. I understand that you appear for the family of the deceased. Miss Hamilton appeared to think that you would expect her to be represented separately."

Mr. Ord said: "Quite so. It is in fact a relief. We are solicitors for Mrs. Hamilton's family—for the Sheldon interests. Had Miss Hamilton come to us, we should have felt compelled to decline."

The words were dryly, not rudely, said, and it may have been from an actual intention of showing that he had meant no personal discourtesy that Mr. Ord added: "I heard, as I came in, that Tom Bellman's been briefed this morning for the police." But Mr. Jellipot took this to mean that his client was to be started on her way to the hangman's shed, and that Ord, Ord & Shaftsbury wished to keep as distant from such contamination as the fact that Lilian Sheldon had married Ada Hamilton's father would enable them to do, and his resentment rose.

Apart from that, the information was ominous, though he was glad to have it. Tom Bellman was a criminal barrister who was frequently briefed for the Crown in important cases, but not usually in such as required subtle or difficult advocacy. Tom Bellman would take his case as a bull charges a gate. He might be out-argued on points of law, or pulled up at times by a judge of equal personality to his own, but he could talk to a jury in a way that they understood, and his reputation for shrewd remorseless bullying in cross-examination would often keep a prisoner out of the box who would have told his tale, either true or false, if he had been faced by a milder counsel.

If it had been decided to brief Tom Bellman since yesterday afternoon, it meant that the Crown had decided that murder had been done, and that there could be no defence that his sledge hammer would not be equal to batter down.

Showing no sign of these thoughts, Mr. Jellipot replied: "Oh, Bellman, is it? Thanks for telling me. I think I met him once at a dinner—perhaps two years ago. I thought him rather an—an emphatic man."

The conversation went no further, for at that moment Mr. Lamson entered and took his seat, and a minute later, while the jury were being sworn, Tom Bellman also appeared, with the instructing solicitor at his side, and their attendant clerks behind them.

CHAPTER IX.

SIR LIONEL TIPSHIFT was in the box. "There was indication," he was saying, "of a paralysis of the heart muscle which must have preceded, and indeed been the immediate cause of death.

"The condition was new to me, excepting only as I had observed it in post-mortems upon non-human subjects which had been subjected to injections of a little-known drug which has been recently used as a local anæsthetic and which, with your permission, I will call X."

"Do I understand, Sir Lionel," the coroner interposed, "that you regard it as contrary to public policy that it should be openly mentioned?"

"I suggest that it may be undesirable."

"Very well. It is possible that there may be no necessity to do so. Pray go on."

"I proposed to Dr. Burfoot, who assisted me at the post-mortem, that portions of the liver and spleen, in which organs such a drug would most certainly be found, should be sent in sealed jars to separate analysts—Drs. Campbell Richie and Victor Southfield—so that the necessary tests should be made."

"Is that the usual procedure under such circumstances?"

"No. It was an additional precaution."

"And the result was that both these analyses discovered the drug X to be present in fatal quantities?"

"Yes."

"In view of which, can you state definitely that the drug X was the cause of Mrs. Hamilton's death?"

"I should say that it is beyond reasonable doubt."

The coroner's glance travelled along the row of legal gentlemen before him. "Any questions you would like to put to the witness?" he asked.

Mr. Bellman looked the indifference he felt. He was satisfied that Sir Lionel's evidence, as it had been fluently given in reply to his apposite questions, was of an impregnable quality. Experienced barrister and experienced witness were equally indifferent to any attack that might be launched by solicitors less practised than themselves upon the battlefields of the criminal courts.

Mr. Ord shook his head.

Mr. Jellipot rose diffidently. "This mysterious drug," he said, "this drug X—is one to which you had been giving special attention of late, apart from which you might not have suspected its presence?"

"Yes."

"Rather a curious coincidence, is it not?"

"Scarcely that, I should say."

"It is not scheduled as a poison?"

"At present, no."

"Dr. Burfoot had previously certified without hesitation that this was a case of natural death from old-standing disease?"

"So I am informed. I may say that I think any doctor might have done so on the facts as he knew them. I feel sure that I should have done the same."

"Thank you, Sir Lionel."

Mr. Jellipot sat down with a feeling that he would have done better to have said nothing.

It might be well, in a case of this kind, and as a general procedure, to challenge every statement in every possible way, and it was true that there is little an expert witness can say that another expert will not contradict with an equal confidence. But Mr. Jellipot had had no opportunity either to call conflicting experts or to have the medical evidence reviewed. He had had no possible time to read up the authorities himself, and he was therefore unprepared for a duel with such a witness.

Beside which, he could not deny to his own mind that though the element of coincidence might be present, its importance was discounted by the fact that Sir Lionel had recognized the fatal symptoms *before* the analyses which had justified his suspicions Mr. Jellipot was not one of those lawyers who are never satisfied except by the sound of their own tongues, and it appeared to him that if by any means it might be possible to defend his client from the suspicion which was surely settling upon her, with the slow relentless certainty which is usual to English judicial process, it would not be that of disputing over the drug which had caused Mrs. Hamilton's death.

He was conscious also that it was a doubtful policy for him, as Ada Hamilton's solicitor, to appear anxious to refute this evidence. There is a folly known as fitting the cap to your own head, and Sir

Lionel Tipshift, a man of fine presence, a bald height of forehead, and a pleasant resonant voice, gave his evidence with an aloof air of disinterested impartiality which was of more value to impress a jury than all the expert knowledge that he certainly had.

So Mr. Jellipot felt that it would have been as well, if not better, to have kept his seat, and when Doctors Richie and Southfield followed Sir Lionel into the box, and gave their evidence in technical language not always easy to follow, they were allowed to go without any questions from him.

After that came a surprise. Mr. Lamson summoned Inspector Combridge to his desk, and there was an interval of some minutes while they talked together in voices too low to be audible to the curious court. And then the coroner turned to the jury to say: "Gentlemen, as it would, in any event, be impossible to complete the case today, and an adjournment will be necessary, I have decided that this will be a convenient point at which to take it.

"The adjournment will be *sine die*, by which you will understand that your attendance will not be required unless you receive a further summons stating the time and place at which I shall require your assistance."

Ada Hamilton, being unused to the procedure on such occasions, and ignorant both of the law and custom by which they were ruled, heard these words with bewilderment, and rose mechanically rather than with any clear purpose, in harmony with the movements that were now stirring around her.

"What does it mean?" she asked Mr. Jellipot, as he also rose, and turned toward her. "Is it all over now?"

"I'm afraid we mustn't expect that. It means that the coroner won't do anything more at present, because Inspector Combridge is taking it in hand.... It means, among other things, that we must trace the writer of that letter as promptly as possible.... You had better go home now, and come to my office, say at eleven-thirty tomorrow morning. I don't suppose there'll be much done in any direction before then."

Miss Hamilton said she would do that, and left the court, still in some bewilderment as to the legal significance of what had occurred.

She was relieved that she had not been called upon to go into the box herself, which is an ordeal most women dread, even in matters in which they are not directly concerned; but she was becoming conscious of the remorseless indifferent leisureliness of the law, that, like a slow patient bloodhound, pursued its prey without heeding the pace of its victim's flight, be it fast or slow, knowing that it was on a scent that it would not lose. Was it on her own track that the bloodhound commenced to bay? It was a thought she could not avoid after the conversation she had had with Mr. Jellipot the night before, and it stirred her heart to a panic fear.

She did not think that anyone, even Inspector Combridge, had any wish to cause her trouble or grief. Indeed, it was he who had recommended her to the lawyer in whom she had come to think already that the hope of her safety lay. But there was no comfort in that. The bloodhound had no animosity toward the stranger on whose scent he was put. He did what he was told, being the tool of a greater power. And so it was with these men who fulfilled the law. Coroner, jury, detectives, lawyers, and judges, they were all like the tools of a blind terrible force which they could not rule if they would, any more than she. They might have no animosity against her. They might be sorry for what they did. But they would make no difference for that.... She had read that they would even be kind to a man they would hang in the next hour: that they would give him a special choice of foods for his breakfast before he died. There seemed something monstrous in that. Something more unnatural, more sinister, than if they had torn him to pieces in a heat of indignation against whatever wrong he had done.... To be kind to a man whom you will inexorably combine to hang in the next hour!

But they would say he is not to be hanged by them, but by the black shadow of law that is over all.... To be hanged! With a sudden shock of fearful, incredulous, realization, she saw it as a shadow that darkened over *herself*, that reached for her with grasping hands.... That was what Mr. Jellipot's hints and questions had meant her to understand. Step by step they would go on to decide that her stepmother had been poisoned...that no one but she could have done it...that it must be she...that it *was* she. They would say that she had done it for the money her father left.... They would do all this in a slow, considerate, impersonal way, and would treat her kindly before she died. For they hang women as well as men. They would do all this unless Mr. Jellipot should find some means to turn them aside, which she saw that she would be powerless to do....

She became aware that she had reached home with this fear stunning her mind, though she could not recall the way she had come, or that she had opened the door. But the telephone was ringing urgently now, and she took the receiver up with a shaking hand.

The voice she heard brought her back to the normal current of life, as though she were sharply waked from a fearful dream. It said: "That you, dear? Yes, I thought you'd be back by now.... Yes, I dropped in at the court.... No, you couldn't have seen me, because I hurried back here as soon as I saw that the old josser was closing down for the day. I thought you might like to go on the river this afternoon, and I'd come back and clear up so that I could get off by when you would be ready.... Or of course I'll call for you, if you like.... Very well, that will be better still. Victoria Underground, at three prompt. Main entrance. I'll be there a little before. Goodbye, darling. Be as quick as you can."

"All right, Phil, I'll be there."

The nightmare fear had passed with the cheerful, confident words, and she was back in the waking world. It couldn't *really* happen to her.

CHAPTER X.

MR. JELLIPOT and Inspector Combridge were alike in thinking that the discovery of the author of the anonymous letter had become the central factor of the situation with which, from their different angles, they were required to deal. They differed only in the intention with which they looked to a common goal.

Inspector Combridge regarded the case as having reached a stage with which he was continually familiar, and at which his real difficulties would commence. He had demonstrated a crime. He had identified the criminal beyond serious doubt. He had still to obtain evidence of guilt in a form in which it could be presented to a jury, with the assurance that it would win the verdict that his own credit required.

He had arrived at the cause of death. Poison. That, he thought, was a fact that even Mr. Jellipot's tenacious ingenuity would be unable to shake. He could show motive and opportunity. That was much, but he knew it to be far less than enough. There was the possibility of self-destruction to be eliminated. There w as the means by which the poison could have been—if possible the actual proof of how it had been—obtained to discover before he would reach a stage at which he could even ask for a warrant to be made out.

He was not depressed or discouraged by any confronting difficulty in obtaining the proofs he needed. Such problems had been his daily routine during fifteen years of growing responsibility, and of the confidence of his superiors. And the fact that the drug was new and little known might seem an obstacle at the first, but would probably prove to be of an opposite value by limiting the extent of the enquiries which were involved.

But, before all, he saw the letter as the key by which the truth would be reached. For of one thing there could be no reasonable doubt. *The man who wrote it knew.*

He had not made so wild a guess as it would have been had he no knowledge of what he wrote. He was not found as yet, and the prospect of finding him might not have been greatly increased by enlisting Mr. Jellipot's efforts on the same trail, but the inspector did not doubt, now that he had a definite case of murder with which to deal, that patience and industry would have the reward that they had often brought him before.

Mr. Jellipot saw the letter in the same light, as being at the core of the problem he sought to solve. He differed only in regarding it as a key to the truth without allowing himself to assume that it would supply proof of his client's guilt.

On the contrary, he had deliberately resolved to assume her innocence, telling himself that it was only on that presumption that he could do justice to the possibility—however small—that it might be actually true. If she were innocent, then there must be another explanation of what had occurred, and, by exhaustion of the logical possibilities of the case, that solution should not be overlooked. But he saw, like the inspector, that if the origin of the letter could be discovered, his problem would be likely to take a much simpler form.

He spent a wakeful night in speculations the improbabilities of which were evident, even while they were formed in his active brain; and he had got no further than to decide that he would make no decision until he had had another talk with Miss Hamilton when he arrived at his office next morning, and was informed almost immediately that Inspector Combridge had called to see him.

He was not entirely surprised, in view of the fact that the inspector had introduced Ada Hamilton, and of the friendship which existed between them, for he saw it to be mutually necessary that they should define the degree of confidence which should exist between them if he should continue to represent the interests of the suspected woman.

"It's this Hamilton case," the inspector said at once, as he sat down. "I thought I'd like to know whether you're throwing it up after what we heard yesterday?"

"My instructions," Mr. Jellipot replied, with his usual quiet geniality, "were to trace the writer of an anonymous letter which has caused a great deal of trouble already, and appears likely to cause more. I did not observe anything in the evidence to which we listened yesterday to reduce the importance of that enquiry…. Indeed," he concluded, with some increased animation, as though a further light came to his mind while he spoke, "rather the other way!"

The inspector allowed a slight smile to disturb his usual seriousness. "Oh, well," he said, "if you're going to take it like that!"

"The enquiry," Mr. Jellipot continued with a resumed placidity, "is, as I pointed out to you at the time, outside the compass of my usual professional activities, and it was therefore one which I undertook with reluctance, and at which I am quite likely to fail. But unless Miss Hamilton prefers to place it in more competent hands—which I should approve—I do not see how I can decline the assistance which I have undertaken to give."

"The question is," the inspector asked bluntly, "how far we can work together, as we shall both be on the same track?"

"Miss Hamilton is due to call here in about twenty minutes, and I should suppose that she will be at least as punctual as ladies usually are. Would you care to remain, so that we can have a frank conference together?"

Inspector Combridge stared at the solicitor in a moment of puzzled doubt, though he was not usually a slow-witted man. Was the proposal seriously meant? Anyway, it was something he could not do. "No," he said, "I don't think I could do that."

As Mr. Jellipot regarded him silently, he added: "I suppose you mean that I've answered my own question?"

"Yes. I should say you have."

"Well, if it's understood that we're on opposite sides, I don't see why—"

The tone was one of conciliation and it is improbable that Inspector Combridge was about to say anything of an unfriendly character, but the sentence was never finished, for Mr. Jellipot interrupted with more warmth than he often showed.

"My dear Combridge, I cannot possibly pass that word. We are not on opposite sides at all! I am an officer of the court, and it is my desire that the guilty shall be punished, and that the innocent shall go free."

"Oh, well, of course, you won't expect me to say that I want anything different from that! But all the same—"

"The point," Mr. Jellipot, who had quickly regained his usual equanimity, replied, "is sufficiently obvious."

The inspector rose to go. "I don't think," he said, "that I should care to meet Miss Hamilton here, and talk to her as though I'm taking her part, but I think she should be asked to make a statement of what she knows; and if you'd care to make an appointment, you could be present, to see we don't put anything in that isn't fair to herself—"

"If I should advise my client to make a signed statement to the police? But that is what I shall be particularly unlikely to do."

Inspector Combridge went at this without further words, and, as he did so, Miss Hamilton was shown in through the opposite door, as had happened two days before, but on this occasion she did not enter alone.

CHAPTER XI.

"THIS," Miss Hamilton said, "is Mr. North. He thought he'd like to come with me, if you wouldn't mind."

"Not at all," Mr. Jellipot said with sincerity, "I am pleased to meet him."

He looked at a man upon whom his thoughts had fixed in the night as one of the three among whom the coroner's anonymous correspondent would almost certainly be found. The fact of this visit did not decrease that suspicion. But it would certainly save his time, and might radically alter the procedure on which he had decided, if all the suspects would be sufficiently obliging to come to him.

He now observed a young man on whom Nature had bestowed little original beauty, and to which accident had added a broken nose. He was short, thick, with black straight hair, and heavy black eyebrows over small deep-set eyes of no certain colour, set in a sallow face. He was well-groomed, and gave Mr. Jellipot, at this first glance, the impression of a man who would be competent to carry through what he undertook: who would push his way through a crowd who might be ruthless in what he did for his own release, if he should be caught in a closing trap. On the whole, this first impression did nothing to lessen the suspicion already formed.

"I thought," Philip North said, "that I might be able to tell you some things that you ought to know."

"I shall be very glad to hear them. At present I know very little about this matter. Very little indeed."

(By all means let the dentist talk, if he were willing to do so. It would be far better than asking questions, which would reveal, more or less, what was in his mind. But as to believing what he heard—well, he must not be prejudiced either way.)

"I was in court yesterday morning, and I heard Sir Lionel Tipshift's evidence. There's no doubt about the drug he meant. It's a preparation put on the market recently by a firm that specializes in anæsthetics. It isn't sold in the chemists' shops, and I should think it would be hard to obtain by anyone outside the professions. The firm circularizes dentists and supplies it direct. It isn't on the scheduled list of poisons, as Sir Lionel said, but on the other hand its existence isn't generally known."

"It has probably been advertised in your periodicals?"

"Yes. And there have been articles and correspondence about it."

"Which would give it a form of publicity which might come under the notice of almost anyone?"

"Yes. To a limited extent."

Mr. Jellipot became aware that he was himself altering the character of the interview. He had seen the advantage of letting his visitor talk freely, but he had, from professional habit, already begun to interpose questions which had obstructed the natural course of the narrative. He said: "I am sorry I interrupted. Pray go on, Mr. North. I expect you have yourself had some clinical opportunities of observing how this drug acts as a local anæsthetic?"

"Yes. We were one of the first to try it—that is, after the dental hospitals had taken it up. Our Dr. Addison is always keen on anything new. And, on the whole, we have been very well satisfied with its results for single extractions. But we found it unsuitable for more extensive use. If it were injected in more than infinitesimal quantities, patients would complain that the jaw was numbed for some time subsequently. We had one case that approached temporary paralysis, and after that Mr. Lobbs didn't favour its use, particularly as there were reports of similar experiences at the hospitals.

"But we've still got some of it in stock, and when Sir Lionel Tipshift spots it as the cause of Mrs. Hamilton's death (and his opinion's about the best you can have: you can't go beyond that), and Miss Hamilton having been at the office—well, someone's almost sure to put the two things together, and I thought we'd better come and have a straight talk with you at once, and see what can be done."

"It is the wisest course you could adopt," Mr. Jellipot said, with the inevitable reservation that he was presuming the innocence of both his visitors, of which he was less than sure.

"It is impossible for any solicitor to do justice to a position of this difficulty unless he be fully informed of every circumstance bearing upon it, however trivial it may seem to be."

"Well, we're here to talk. I suppose I needn't tell you that Ada didn't give Mrs. Hamilton any of the stuff. Of course, that's absurd. But she says more than that. She says she never had anything to do with it at all. She says she couldn't possibly have taken any of it home with her, and I don't believe Mrs. Hamilton ever came up the stairs at Corbin Street in her life. And if so, we've got to trace it to some other source, however queer it may seem to be."

"I am sure you recognize, Mr. North, that it is immensely improbable that such a coincidence should occur as that there should be two channels through which this obscure poison could be introduced into Mrs. Hamilton's house."

"Yes. I suppose it is. But Ada says she's quite sure. You can't get beyond that."

Mr. Jellipot turned his glance upon Miss Hamilton, who had not spoken as yet. Her face looked white and strained, and she had kept her eyes fixed upon her companion the while he spoke, as though relying dumbly upon him to pull her through. Had she been the foolish tool of a crime which she might not even have understood at the time, and was she now looking to the actual criminal to guard her from the danger to which she had fallen under the influence of his stronger will?

Or was she a poisoner who relied upon his affection, and her own hardy lying, to draw her back from the edge of the pit upon which she stood?

Or—and perhaps most likely of all—were they involved to an equal depth in the plot which had seemed so safe, and which, but for that anonymous letter, would have succeeded so simply? A plot by which the girl would have been relieved from the companionship of a woman she most probably hated, as having taken her father's affections, and who held possession of the wealth which she herself would know better how to spend, and by which they would have been free to marry and share the spoils of their secret crime?

With these doubts in a mind which he was still resolved to keep wide open to whatever further evidence might appear, Mr. Jellipot asked: "Could you swear definitely that, so far as you are aware, Miss Hamilton was not concerned with the anæsthetics used in your surgeries, nor even cognizant of them?"

"No, you couldn't go quite as far as that. She'd have to admit that she wrote out the orders for them, and checked the accounts for payment. And I've talked to her about this one myself more than once, though I can't say she took much notice of what I said."

"I never listened to Phil when he talked shop after we'd got away. I wasn't interested enough."

There was a tone of sincerity—or was it desperation?—in this interjected protest. Mr. Jellipot said: "Yes, I expect you were more interested in other things," and turned his attention back to Mr. North to ask: "I expect you sometimes called yourself at Mrs. Hamilton's residence?"

"Yes. I went there to dinner two or three times."

"And Mrs. Hamilton welcomed you as her stepdaughter's friend?"

"Oh, yes. She was always friendly and hospitable."

"Did she ever discuss drugs or anæsthetics with you at any time?"

"Never at all."

"Or did you discuss them before her?"

"No, never at all. It isn't a professional custom to talk about such matters. We should be talking about our patients next thing, if we did that. And it isn't a subject that people like. When they meet us socially they prefer to forget us in our professional capacity. Of course, talking to Ada was different between ourselves."

"Yes, I see. Then you are absolutely unable to suggest any way in which this drug could have been conveyed to Mrs. Hamilton from your Corbin Street office, or how it could have been taken by her either deliberately or by inadvertence?"

"No. And we say it didn't come from Corbin Street, whether people believe it or not.... I can't suggest anything except that Dr. Burfoot may have tried it on her, and made a mistake that he isn't anxious to let out."

"It is a possibility," Mr. Jellipot admitted, "which has been in my own mind, and which, on the information you have given me, we may be able to check. But, apart from that, you have no suggestion to make?"

"Not except that I should be glad to see the letter that's at the bottom of all the fuss. If I could tell the handwriting it might get us a long way."

"So it might. But I should not advise you to anticipate any result from your own inspection. If you can identify the handwriting, it will be more than those who are expert in these matters have been able to do.

"But there will be no difficulty in arranging for you to see it. It has, I believe, been already handed over by Mr. Lamson to the police.... Suppose you come in on Monday, say at 3:00 P.M.—can you manage that?—and I will arrange to go with you to Scotland Yard, which will, I suggest, be better than that you should go there alone?"

"Yes, I'll do that. I suppose Ada'd better come too?"

"No. It will not be necessary.... I think, Miss Hamilton, it would be better for you to go home, and leave Mr. North and me to do the worrying over this matter. You can be sure that the truth will come out at last. But don't talk to anyone, particularly not to the police, however kind—or otherwise—they may seem to be. You need say no more than that I have told you to refer them to me."

They went away, leaving Mr. Jellipot well content. He did not think that Philip North would be of much assistance in identifying the letter, but he thought he might talk rather differently if Miss Hamilton were not there; and if everyone concerned would be good enough to walk into his office and be equally voluble—well, there oughtn't to be much trouble in finding out where the truth lay.

CHAPTER XII.

MR. NORTH arrived punctually on Monday at 3:00 P.M., and Mr. Jellipot told him at once that he had arranged for them to attend together at Scotland Yard to inspect the letter at four; but that is no evidence that he could not have fixed the appointment for half an hour earlier, had he preferred to do so.

The fact was that he had contrived an interval for the conversation which he regarded as the most important part of the afternoon's programme, and he was pleased to find that Mr. North was as ready of speech as he had been at the earlier interview.

"I thought," he began in the courteous, almost deprecating tone which was habitual to him, except only when his well-regulated emotions would occasionally escape control, "that as you are kind enough to interest yourself in this matter, the short interval might not be wasted, if we find ourselves able to discuss it with a freedom which might be difficult in Miss Hamilton's presence."

"Well, I'm here to do that. It seems to me that she may find herself in a bad jam."

"In such matters it is my observation that the innocent seldom have any prolonged anxiety. Speaking in the strictest confidence, Mr. North, and remembering that I am acting entirely in Miss Hamilton's interests, will you tell me if you have any reason to doubt the truth of what actually occurred?"

The question was somewhat ambiguously put, and, even so, Mr. Jellipot did not frame it without some doubt of its fundamental propriety troubling his mind. But it was asked at least as much to test Philip North himself as the conduct of the girl whom it more directly concerned.

He found that the question was met with a puzzled and angry frown. "She didn't poison Mrs. Hamilton, if you mean that."

The words were blunt, even to rudeness, but Mr. Jellipot showed no sign of offence. "Whatever my question may be fairly taken to imply," he said mildly, "which is a point we need not turn aside to discuss, I am pleased to know that your confidence in my client is so complete. It increases my own confidence in my ability to solve the difficult problem which I have undertaken on her behalf.... Mr. North, I am sure you will appreciate the importance, in Miss Hamilton's own interest, of my being correctly informed on all the details of these events. Will you tell me further whether you would say that Miss Hamilton is always exactly truthful in what she says?"

"She can fib a bit now and then."

"Normally, or only when under exceptional stress?"

"Oh, when women do. They're mostly the same about that, as far as they come my way."

Mr. Jellipot, a man of precise thought and of words carefully picked, hesitated to take this view. "You may have been unfortunate," he replied, "in the ladies whose society you have been privileged to enjoy. But I suppose you allude to minor and perhaps venial inaccuracies of speech, such as may be induced by courtesy or diffidence, or may even be of a sportive kind."

"Yes, I suppose that's about it."

Mr. Jellipot changed the subject to ask: "I suppose you have no suggestion to make as to who the writer of the anonymous letter might possibly be?"

"No. I wish I had. I think that's about the biggest mystery of the whole thing."

"You would not agree that it was most probably written by someone in your own offices?"

"I can see that it looks that way, more or less, but all the same I don't think that it was. I think I know them too well."

"Dr. Addison?"

Mr. North looked surprised, not being aware of the knowledge of the Corbin Street staff which Mr. Jellipot had already obtained. "Yes," he said, "I know what you mean, but he's not that sort all the same."

"Well, you know them better than I. But people will sometimes do some surprising things.... Suppose we take Mrs. Hamilton's relatives, if you feel you can give your own office a clean bill. What about Vincent Hamilton?"

Mr. North looked surprised again. He asked: "Did Ada tell you about him? What did she say?"

"If my memory serves me correctly, she did not mention him at all. But I have heard of him from another source."

"Well, I'll say one thing. You haven't lost very much time. As to Vincent, he's just a crook. There isn't much that he wouldn't do, if he thought he could land it safely, and keep just outside the prison doors. It beats me what a girl like Ada could ever see—but there's no need to go into that now. But I should say it would be just in his line.

"Only, why should he? It doesn't make sense somehow. Not unless he'd poisoned the old lady himself; and he'd no quarrel with her. I should say it was rather the other way."

Mr. Jellipot, listening to these exclamatory remarks, felt that he was learning much, including some things that he had not guessed. But he preferred to finish one argument before he commenced the next.

"I don't think the absence of motive would be the real difficulty," he replied, "because if, by whatever means, he could place upon Miss Hamilton the guilt of her stepmother's death, she would be legally barred from inheriting under her father's will, and there is a suggestion that he may be the next of kin.

"The real difficulty is of another kind. The letter would be pointless, and any temporary trouble it might cause would be abortive in its result, unless there should prove to be substance in the allegation which it contained.

"We must conclude therefore that the writer of the letter was either the criminal himself, or had substantial reason for concluding that the crime had been committed, which, if he did not believe that Miss Hamilton were actually guilty, he hoped to see fastened upon her.

"How far and under what circumstances could Vincent Hamilton have been in that position? That is the problem we have to face, and which you may possibly help me to solve. My only information at present is that he was not near the house at any time during Mrs. Hamilton's illness, nor did he communicate with it in any way."

"I don't see how you could be sure about that."

"I must trust your discretion when I tell you in confidence that he was under the observation of the police."

"Well, that wouldn't be for the first time. I hope they'll put him where he belongs. But I can't see how he comes in here."

"Neither can I. But it's sometimes wonderful how far you get if you go one step at a time.... I can see that you have no admiration for Mr. Vincent. Can you tell me what are Miss Hamilton's feelings toward him, or, more important, what would his feelings be toward her? Would he be likely to want to do her a bad turn if he could?"

"No. It's the other way round. She was engaged to him up to three months ago."

"By whom was it broken off?"

"By her. She couldn't help seeing what a bounder he is."

"Then we may assume that they quarrelled?"

"I suppose they did, more or less."

"So that he might be in a revengeful mood, and disposed to do her an ill turn if he could?"

"I don't know," Mr. North answered doubtfully. "I rather thought he was trying to get round her again."

It was evident that the idea of a revengeful plot did not present itself to Mr. North's mind with convincing force, and Mr. Jellipot recognized that the significance of this attitude was increased by the fact that it arose from no liking for Vincent Hamilton, or doubt that he would be base enough to contrive it. It simply did not fit the facts, as he knew or believed them to be.

Reluctantly, Mr. Jellipot abandoned one of the theories which had seemed to throw a faint ray of possible explanation upon the darkness in which he groped.

"Should you say," he asked, stubbornly continuing to advance his attack from a different angle, "that he had wooed her from genuine affection, or for the sake of the money which she would inherit?"

"I don't know how to answer that. I only met him three or four times, and the last of those was a row. You couldn't tell with a man like him."

"I dare say that most of what you know about him you heard from Miss Hamilton?"

"Yes, that's more or less true. And what I saw. And Mrs. Hamilton said things once or twice."

"Mrs. Hamilton disliked him?"

"Not exactly. She didn't trust him. She knew him too well for that. It was partly through her that the engagement was broken off.... But there was nothing special in that. I should say you'll find plenty of people who don't like Vincent, if you go round looking them up."

"Well, you're one, anyway," Mr. Jellipot said with a smile, as he rose from his desk. "I don't blame you for that. You've told me a good many things that I'm glad to know; but it's time to be moving now."

CHAPTER XIII.

"I SUPPOSE," Philip North asked abruptly, as they were seated in the taxi which Mr. Jellipot had engaged for the two-mile journey from his city office to Scotland Yard, "you thought some of the things I told you this morning won't do Ada any good if they come out?"

"I should have been glad," Mr. Jellipot answered cautiously, "for Miss Hamilton's sake, if you had been able to answer differently in some instances. But it is possible that you mayn't be asked the same questions again, and, in any case, I cannot give you safer advice, even in her own interest, than to give the true facts as fairly and accurately as you can."

"Yes, it ought to be the safe way." The words were spoken without conviction, and a moment later he asked: "It's the law, isn't it, that a man cannot give evidence against his wife?"

"It is the law that he cannot be compelled to do so."

"Well, if he doesn't want to, that comes to the same thing."

"Not precisely."

Mr. Jellipot might have given some practical illustrations of this difference, but at this moment the taxi turned out of Whitehall into New Scotland Yard, and drew up at the entrance to the police headquarters. The visit, so far as its direct object was concerned, was as fruitless as Mr. Jellipot had anticipated. Mr. North inspected the letter, and was unable to make any suggestion as to its authorship: "Anyone," he said, "might make printed capitals like that." And though a handwriting expert would have qualified this statement, and might even have claimed to detect some individualities in the crudely printed characters, it was an opinion with which most people would agree.

Inspector Combridge was also present, and would doubtless have used the occasion to discuss some aspects of the case more fully with Mr. North than he attempted to do, had the dentist not been under Mr. Jellipot's watchful guardianship.

He was already considering him in the light of an accessory, if not the equal accomplice of the actual murderess, though he recognized that his guilt might be more difficult, and perhaps impossible to prove; for if Miss Hamilton, as he was already informed, had herself direct access to the poison which she employed, the necessity for his co-operation did not arise, and only her own confession could involve him in complicity with her, even though he might have contrived and suggested the crime.

"If you have a few minutes to spare," Mr. Jellipot said, "there is one matter I should like to discuss with you, if Mr. North will excuse me."

The inspector replied that his time was at Mr. Jellipot's service, and Philip North having rather reluctantly departed—for there was a matter upon his mind on which he would have liked to consult the solicitor further—Inspector Combridge said: "I don't know that we ought to have let him see it, but we didn't like to refuse, the request coming from you as it did."

It was a view of the matter which Mr. Jellipot frankly admitted to his own mind that he had failed to consider. He said: "I had not thought that there would be any favour in that. I considered that we are both endeavouring to discover who the writer may be, and to that extent we are working to the same end."

"Well, there's no harm done, anyway. I think he told the truth when he said he'd no idea who wrote it. But, if he had, do you think he'd have let it out?"

"In my opinion," Mr. Jellipot said rather stiffly, "he is extremely anxious to find out who the writer is."

"I expect that's true, if he doesn't know. But what I said was that he wouldn't let it out, either to you or me.... I suppose you know that he and the girl are as thick as thieves—or perhaps something a bit worse would be the more accurate word."

"I am aware that Mr. North is very anxious to get at the truth, so that the suspicion which must otherwise be more or less inevitably attached to Miss Hamilton may be entirely removed."

"That's one way of putting it. I suppose you haven't thought that if he could guess who the writer is there might be another murder, rather more likely than not?"

"It is a contingency," Mr. Jellipot admitted frankly, "to which I had not given the consideration which you evidently think it requires."

"Well, we're not letting him out of our sight. So if he gets on the right track he may lead us up to the man we want more likely than not. But perhaps I shouldn't have told you that."

"It is a confidence which I shall respect.... But there was another matter on which I thought we might help each other, or perhaps you'd say that you'd be helping me."

"Well, I'll do anything I properly can. You know that."

"The case, from your point of view, as it now stands, may perhaps be fairly stated in this way: it appears to be certain that Mrs. Hamilton's death resulted from the administration of a certain drug which is in very restricted circulation. Miss Hamilton had access to that drug. She was nursing her stepmother. She had ample opportunities for introducing it into her food or medicine, or perhaps otherwise administering it. She had motive for so doing. The domestics in the house had no such motive, nor, so far as we are at present informed, had they any means of procuring the drug, nor (in all probability) any knowledge of its nature or effects.

"Consequently, you regard Miss Hamilton as the murderess of the elder woman, but you feel that the evidence, though conclusive to your own mind, falls somewhat short of the proof that the law requires, and you wish to strengthen it before making an arrest, which it is not therefore your immediate purpose to do."

"I don't promise anything. But I don't suppose we shall do that till we've got the case a bit more complete. Not so long as she stays where she is now."

"Which I should most certainly advise her to do. But I was not intending to ask you for any promise of that kind. I merely wished to be sure that we understood one another as to how the case looks from the official standpoint."

"Yes. I couldn't have put it better myself. We just want the bit of extra proof that would make a committal certain, and then take her on the rest of the way that poisoners go, and I don't reckon it will be long before we shall be ready to move ahead."

"But you also wish to be quite sure that you are making no mistake. You wish to eliminate any alternative channel by which the drug might possibly have reached Mrs. Hamilton's hands."

"If we saw any alternative we should wish to eliminate it. At present I can't say that we do."

"I can suggest one at least. The drug was advertised in the dental Press. Miss Hamilton might have taken a periodical home, or Mr. North might have laid it down and left it there on one of his visits, and Mrs. Hamilton might have purchased the drug herself as a result of something she read."

"It's a most improbable theory."

"I agree. But it is a possibility, and it is one, I will venture to say, that you had not considered. There may be others."

"Do they say that they took these papers home?"

"I have not discussed such a possibility with either of them. I have only put it to you."

"Well, it's ingenious, but it wouldn't help you much unless you could show that Mrs. Hamilton really purchased the drug."

"No, I don't say that it would."

"What are you going to ask us to do?"

"It is a drug which is prepared by one firm alone. They can only have a very limited number of customers, of whom their books would supply a complete record. They might, or might not, disclose them to me. They will certainly do so to you. I suggest that you should check up on them thoroughly to eliminate the possibility that the drug may have been supplied to Mrs. Hamilton direct, or through some other ascertainable channel."

The inspector considered this prospect rather sourly at first, for he was quick to observe that while it might serve Mr. Jellipot's client, there was no prospect that it would be of service to him in the building up of the case that he had to make, except in a negative way.

Having arrived at a definite conviction of Ada Hamilton's guilt in an experienced mind, he regarded the proposed enquiry as wasted effort in itself, and of a kind which should be undertaken, if at all, by Miss Hamilton's defence rather than the police.

But it was true that he did not wish, either for his own sake or hers, to arrest her if she were an innocent woman, and Mr. Jellipot had suggested a possibility, however remote, which he could not refuse to probe.

"Yes," he said, "I reckon I owe you something for landing the case on to your desk in the way I did. I won't refuse to do that."

"I am extremely obliged, and I am not without hope that something tangible may result."

It was a bargain from which Mr. Jellipot saw at least one tangible gain which it would have been foolish to speak. He knew, even after the assurance he had received, that the question of Ada Hamilton's arrest must have been under discussion, and that the case against her was of such a strength already that it might be resolved, at almost any moment, to place her in the security of a prison cell, with the intention of asking for one of those remands, after formal evidence of arrest, which the magistrates always grant, to allow time for the case to be completed against her.

But now that Inspector Combridge had promised to undertake this eliminating enquiry, Mr. Jellipot felt that he would be likely— indeed certainly, in the absence of some development by which her guilt would be clearly shown—to defer the question of arrest until it had been decided.

His experience in many difficult negotiations during the thirty years of his professional life had taught him that it is a mistake to prolong an interview for one avoidable moment after you have gained the object at which you aim, and so, with the expression of obligation already recorded, he now shook hands very cordially with Inspector Combridge, and returned to his own office.

CHAPTER XIV.

VINCENT HAMILTON lay in bed. It was a good bed, which he was in no hurry to leave. He was one of those men who rise late, if the fates are kind.

They had been kind to Vincent of late, from the day when he had relieved his landlord of £500, of which he considered that he had the more urgent need.

His net profit from that coup had been £330, after he had settled with the gentleman who had done the telephoning, and paid commission on cashing the notes. He had risked most of this during the next week on a single bet, and by all laws of chance and justice it should have gone as easily as it had come into his hands. But, in fact, it had behaved in a contrary way. He had obtained odds of two to nine on a horse which had been first in passing the post, and a smaller bet that he had made the next day with much better odds had been an equal success.

So it came to be that he had a first-floor suite in the Raleigh Hotel, and could put the breakfast tray from his knees, and lie back again in the comfort that leisure knows.

It was true there was a writ for £500 and £5 5s. ("or such a sum as may be allowed on taxation") costs, lying on the dressing table, where he had thrown it carelessly when it had been served upon him the evening before. But he had little trouble for that. Rather the other way. It showed that Mr. Wall had abandoned the idea of criminal proceedings, which the commencement of this civil process would now render it impossible for him to take. That was how Vincent had calculated that it would be; but his confidence had not been absolute enough to relieve him from a faint but never-ceasing fear that he might be touched by a detaining hand, of which that black-printed foolscap sheet had now made an end.

Let Tom Wall waste money on taking a civil judgment, if he would, and if he still had more than he could spend in a better way! Vincent cared little for that. When a man lives by his wits, and has no home, or visible means of support, nor any effects of the kind that can be seized by process of law, he has little to fear from a judgment that only bankruptcy can enforce—a bankruptcy for which Mr. Wall would have to pay.

Vincent Hamilton, considering his present circumstances, had another reason for satisfaction. He had obtained employment of a congenial kind. Regular employment, with the qualification that it might be suspended at any time by the raiding of the Cactus Club, and only resumed when gambling tables should be set up at a new address.

It was employment with certain profit, and no risk. He was not occupying any of these profitable but dangerous positions which are apt to end in heavy police-court fines, such as the owner of the club is not invariably certain to pay, so that the shadow of the cells is always nearer than it is pleasant for it to be. If there should be a raid on the Cactus Club (or perhaps when is a better word, for these incidents are certain to come), Vincent would be no more than one of those unfortunate people whose names are taken, and who are then bailed out, and next morning must listen to the magistrate's admonitions with outward respect, and be fined £1, or perhaps bound over to keep the peace. For Vincent Hamilton's occupation would be to attend as a regular gambling guest who would lay down moderate stakes, and be allowed to win up to £10 or £15 a week for himself, and occasionally larger amounts to be handed back at the evening's close, to demonstrate to all beholders that the wheel was honestly spun.

So if he took an extra hour this morning for dozing and pleasant thought in a bed that was soft and warm, it was no more than he had a good right to do. Fortune and his own excellent wits had united to bring him to where he was, with mind and body at ease, and a conscience that was quiet and well content.

It might be said that such satisfaction showed that his conscience did not exist, but that would be widely wrong. He had a conscience which could be active enough if he should transgress its code, but a fox does not lose sleep for the fate of the rabbit on which he fed, and still less would he feel remorse for the tricks by which he had cheated the eager hounds.

Vincent thought of the futile writ which had been handed to him the night before, and a proverb concerning butter in a dog's mouth came to his mind. His thoughts wandered on to another source of satisfaction—a pleasant prospect the future held—and he became aware that, after all, that £500 might be destined to be repaid. For if he were to receive the benefit of the fortune that Lilian Hamilton had ceased to enjoy, it might not be worth while to have further trouble concerning the smaller sum, and the difficulty of avoiding payment might be more than even his ingenuity would be equal to overcome.

For, with more certain knowledge than Mr. Jellipot had obtained, he knew himself to be Mrs. Hamilton's next of kin, and the significance of that adjourned inquest was clear to a mind stored with more knowledge of the methods of the police than information of better kinds. He watched the newspapers for an announcement of Ada's arrest, which he supposed could not be delayed for many days, even if another anonymous letter did not assist the plodding efforts of the police.

He was interrupted in these comfortable reflections by the ringing of his bedside telephone, and took up the receiver to learn that a Mr. Jellipot wished to see him.

Mr. Hamilton hesitated. He was not one of those narrowly conventional gentlemen who confine their business transactions to stated places or hours, or connect them with the wearing of appropriate clothes. But before receiving callers he preferred to know something both of themselves and the business on which they came. A lively and retentive memory assured him that his large and peculiar acquaintance did not include anyone of Mr. Jellipot's unusual name. And yet—somewhere—he had come across it during the last few days. The subject which had been in his thoughts when the interruption had come assisted his memory to the fact that that had been the name of one of the legal gentlemen who had been representing various interests at the Hamilton inquest, though he could not recall for whom he had been appearing. But the name was not common. Almost certainly it was the same.

It was easy to doubt whether the object of this call was to confer any benefit upon himself, or would be likely to have that result. But he did not keep himself alive and in conditions of considerable though fluctuating comfort, by shirking fences, or trying to bolt from the course. He would see him, with whatever purpose he came, and must trust his wits that he should gain more than he gave away. But it would be impolitic to seem eager to do so. He said: "Well, I'm not up yet. Ask him what his business is."

"He says," the voice of the reception clerk informed him a moment later, "that you would not know him, but that he is a solicitor, and he wishes to see you on urgent business in connection with Mrs. Hamilton's death."

Mr. Jellipot, after commissioning a firm of enquiry agents to undertake investigation on Ada Hamilton's behalf, for which his own office would have been of an inferior competence, had decided that there might be more gain from a direct call upon Vincent Hamilton, whose personality, as it had been unattractively presented to him both by Inspector Combridge and Philip North, intrigued his mind with an instinctive conviction that, even if he were not the writer of the anonymous letter, and even though, on the inspector's reluctant testimony, he had not been near the scene of Mrs. Hamilton's fatal illness, he might yet be able to give information which would point the way to the true solution, if he could be induced to do so.

He saw that a personal interview would enable him to judge the character of the man better than an agent's report, and that, with the exercise of sufficient diplomacy on his side, there was a better prospect of fruitful conversation resulting.

Being determined that he would not allow any consideration either of dignity or etiquette, or of the value of his own time, to obstruct the enquiry he had undertaken, he had come at an early hour, and before proceeding to his own office, on the sound presumption that Vincent Hamilton would not then have left the hotel, and the opportunity for quiet conversation would be better than he would be likely to secure at a later part of the day.

Now as he stood in the hotel office, a trick of sound common to telephone extensions enabled him to hear both ends of the conversation between the hotel clerk and the man he sought. He heard Vincent Hamilton say curtly: "Well, it's not urgent to me. Tell him he'll have to wait, or else call again." And then, as though casually altering his mind: "No, don't tell him that. Tell him he can come up if he likes. I'll give him five minutes before I dress."

"He says he isn't up yet, but he'll see you, sir, all the same if you don't mind," the clerk interpreted politely, and called a pageboy, who led Mr. Jellipot to the lift, for the short journey to Vincent Hamilton's first-floor apartment.

Mr. Jellipot was surprised. He was of too long an experience, and too cautious a disposition, to allow this emotion to appear, but he had not expected to be received in an apartment of such opulent comfort. Inspector Combridge, in giving him the address of the Raleigh, had said nothing of the quality of the hotel itself, or of the nature of the accommodation that Mr. Hamilton had retained. Mr. Jellipot felt that it confirmed the wisdom of his decision to see with his own eyes rather than to trust the reports of others.

He was surprised also, though to a less extent, by the appearance of the man he met. Vincent Hamilton had not risen to greet his visitor. He leaned back comfortably against the heaped pillows of a double bed, wearing a dressing-gown of crimson silk, and looking younger and more handsome in the subdued light of a room in which the curtains were still undrawn than had he been exposed to the glare of the outer day.

"Good morning," he said, pleasantly enough, but without the mistake of any pronounced geniality, "I understand that you want to see me about some business connected with Mrs. Hamilton's death?"

"There is a matter," Mr. Jellipot said, "on which I thought you might be able, and felt sure that you must be willing, to help my client, and which I felt to be less suitable for correspondence than a personal interview."

"Well, you might push those things off the chair, and sit down. Anywhere'll do. You must excuse an informal reception, but if you'd rung me up to let me know you'd like to give me an early call—"

Mr. Jellipot observed himself to be rebuked in a way that he could not resent, and without any rudeness of manner emphasizing the implication of the remark. He considered that if Mr. Hamilton were equally adroit in conversational exchanges of more serious kind, he had met an opponent whom it might not be easy to overcome.

He had been a bare minute in the room, but he could understand already Inspector Combridge's baffled exasperation. He could appreciate the bitter jealousy of the broken-nosed Philip North for this debonair and plausible rival, which had even survived Ada's final preference for his more solid virtues. He could realize Ada's infatuation, and the possibility that, even if she might no longer have hesitation between them, she might have moods of regret for that which Vincent was, and Philip could never be.

These things were easy to see, but the disposition of the man before him was a more difficult guess. He had found with others more or less of the same type, to whom finesse and lying become a routine, that where they will meet subtlety with subtlety, guile with guile, they may recognize a direct sincerity and respond to it with equal candour. He said simply: "It was only this morning that I decided that it would be best to see you myself, and as there is no time to lose, I thought that I would take the chance that you would not have gone out before I could get here."

"Well, you've caught me, all right. I suppose you wouldn't mind telling me how you knew where I was to be found, if you only thought of calling a few hours ago? I've been here two days now, and it hadn't occurred to me to send you the address."

Mr. Jellipot, who habitually avoided the clumsiness of lying, saw the wisdom of a frank rather than an evasive answer.

"I telephoned Inspector Combridge before I left home this morning, and got it from him."

"You thought the police would be sure to know?"

"I knew that Inspector Combridge is enquiring into the circumstances of Mrs. Hamilton's death, and that he would be likely to be in touch with those most nearly related to her."

"That all?"

"Not exactly. Inspector Combridge had mentioned you to me. He told me that a Mr. Wall had been to them to make a complaint against you which, after investigation, they had declined to take up."

Vincent Hamilton showed neither surprise nor annoyance at these explanations. He laughed slightly.

"So I heard. Mr. Wall ought to have had more sense. So you're acting for the police in this matter of Mrs. Hamilton's death?"

"No. Rather the contrary. I am acting for Ada Hamilton, against whom they are inclined to entertain a suspicion which I wish to remove."

"Well, we're friends, Ada and I. I'll do anything for her that I can. And if you're good enough for her, you ought to be good enough for me too.... There's a summons, or whatever you call it, lying on the dressing-table. It's from that gentleman who tried going to the police.... Yes, over there. You might take it for me, and lead him the usual dance. There's a fiver over there too, under the hair-brush. You might take that for any out-of-pockets you have to pay. But I'd see you right any time. I always stand by those who are on my side, even if I sometimes leave the other fellow feeling a bit sore. You can't fill your pocket without someone else's being a bit lighter. But everyone doesn't have the sense to see that."

"No," Mr. Jellipot agreed, "I suppose not." He had moved over to the dressing-table, and picked up the writ, which he scrutinized with habitual care, without observing any superficial irregularity, such as will rejoice a defending solicitor's heart.

It was an unexpected and unwelcome development. He had no inclination to defend Vincent Hamilton in his semi-criminal complications. Inspector Combridge had already drawn his highly respectable office into acting for a young woman against whom a sensational charge of murder would probably be brought within the next week. But it was not therefore to become busy upon the affairs of all the crooks in her peculiar family, and perhaps, after that, to extend its activities for the protection of their too-numerous friends. The fatal nature of the first downhill step, on which moralists have discoursed from the dawn of time!

But Mr. Jellipot saw that it would do nothing to advance the errand on which he came if he should refuse to do the service which he was asked, and which had in itself a significance which he was glad to perceive, for it must surely imply that Mr. Hamilton saw no probability of future complication arising from the fact that Ada and he would be depending upon the same legal adviser—unless, of course, it were a device to buy or bamboozle him to be Vincent Hamilton's tool, in which case he thought that Vincent would be the one most likely to regret the attempt.

Apart from that, he had the trained instinct which made it as natural for him to nurse a new-born writ to the maturity of contested action as for a midwife to cradle a child. He asked: "When did you get this? Last night? I will enter an appearance for you in due course, and after that there will be time to discuss whether there be any substantial defence, or what terms of settlement may be proposed."

"Then that's that," Mr. Hamilton said with finality, feeling a natural satisfaction in having obtained the services of an obviously respectable lawyer to defend an action which must otherwise have gone by default, or been placed in the hands of one of those firms whose own status is apt to be indicative of that of the clients they defend in the civil, and more often in the criminal, courts. "And now about Ada. I don't know what help you can want from me, but if you haven't made up your mind whether she poisoned Lilian, I can put you on the right bet.

"Ada didn't do it, because she isn't the sort, and no one but a policeman whose skull's as thick as his boots would ever think that she did. She hasn't the brains. She hasn't the disposition. She hasn't the guts. She could always tell a good lie, and look as innocent as a cat, and I don't say that if she got in a tight squeeze she'd be overcareful how she got out. She thinks she's a bit smart, and a bit gay, but what she really is you can tell by her planning to spend her life with one of the dullest swine that ever sported a broken nose.

"And, beside that, she'd got nothing to gain that was worth the risk, or even the fag of planning it out, which, you can take it from me, she wouldn't have nerve to do. She was planning to marry Philip North, who's doing quite well enough for a start, and Lilian liked the match much better than if she'd had the sense to be going to marry a better man, and would have given her any money in reason she chose to ask.

"No, if anyone poisoned Lilian, which you ought to know better than I, it wasn't Ada, and you've got to look somewhere else if you want to end at the right address."

Mr. Jellipot listened with interest to this declamation, which he had no disposition to interrupt. He was usually willing to let the other man talk. And though he was not disposed to regard Vincent as an apostle of simple truth, he thought that there was sincerity in his emphatic assertion of Ada's innocence, to which he was the more inclined because some of the arguments he now heard had already entered his own mind with almost convincing force.

But if Vincent were not only assured of her innocence but anxious to convert others to the same opinion, was it reasonable to regard him as the author of a letter which had been intended to cast suspicion upon her? A letter written by someone who, if not the actual criminal, had a private knowledge of the crime before any other suspicion had been aroused.

The answer appeared evident. And, if that were so, he was baffled again in his pursuit both of the anonymous letter-writer and the criminal, and could take consolation only from the added confidence in Ada's innocence which he had gained, and the reflection that each possibility which he eliminated must bring him nearer to the elusive truth.

"I am glad," he said, "that you agree with opinions regarding Miss Hamilton's innocence which I had already formed. It gives me the greater confidence in asking for any help you can give in clearing her from the suspicion of such a crime. I suppose that you will have heard of the anonymous letter from which all this trouble began?"

"Yes, I've heard something of that. I can't say I know just what it contained."

Mr. Jellipot quoted it with verbatim accuracy, which may not be considered surprising, it being a short document, and having been much in his mind. Vincent said: "Well, whoever it was, he seems to have touched the spot, at least as to how Lilian died. What about North, if you're asking guesses from me?"

"I'm not exactly asking guesses. I hoped you might be able to give me some information which would turn enquiry into the right channel.... Of course, I have considered Mr. North. It is a case in which no one who was in contact with the case can safely be overlooked. But I don't think it was he. We may also notice—though of course it would not alter the facts—that it would be extremely difficult, apart from evidence of which we have at present no indication—to connect Mr. North with it in any way without the presumption of conspiracy arising between Miss Hamilton and himself."

"Yes, I suppose that's the snag. Still, it's an idea. What about the maids in the house?"

"I understand that the police have questioned them, and consider that they are outside reasonable suspicion. Miss Hamilton also, whose interest it would be to disclose anything of a contrary nature, takes the same view. There is the improbability, among others, that they would even have known of the existence of the drug in question. In that connection, in which your own observation, as an occasional visitor to the house—"

"I have not been a recent visitor."

"No. But before. The point is, did you happen to see any periodicals connected with dentistry lying about, from the contents of which Mrs. Hamilton—or anyone else—might have gained knowledge of the drug?"

"Would that be a point for Ada, or on the other side of the slate?"

"As I am acting solely as Miss Hamilton's solicitor, you cannot serve her better than by giving me any facts within your own knowledge accurately, without hesitation as to how they may be construed. But I should say that it would be a point in her favour, as showing that others in the house might have had knowledge of the drug as well as herself."

"Yes, I see that. There was a paper—the *Surgeon-Dentist* I think it's called—that used to be frequently lying about the house. I've had Ada reading it more than once when she'd have been better occupied talking to me. When she got thick with North, she took an interest in his work, which was a natural thing for her to do."

Mr. Jellipot felt that he had got all that he asked, and a bit more. He would have been better satisfied with the reply had he not remembered Ada's contrary assurances, and Philip North's confirmation. But he only said: "Thank you. That is what I was anxious to know. Beyond that, is there anything you can tell me which might assist toward the discovery of the one by whom the letter was written?"

"Not except what I've said already, that it's someone in the house, more likely than not. You could put the odds on that at fifty to one, and it would still be a bet that it would be better to leave alone.

"But the fact is that I stopped going there about two months ago. I used to be engaged to Ada—I've no doubt you've been told that—and when she chucked me for North, I took the hint that the less I called the better pleased everyone would be likely to be. But for that, I might have seen a bit more, and you'd probably have been wondering whether I were not the villain you want to find.

"But you can tell Ada from me that, if she thinks I can help, I'll come up to the house, and do anything that I can."

For which offer, without much expectation that it would be accepted, or would have any useful result if it were, Mr. Jellipot thanked him, and left in even greater dubiety than he had been when he entered the hotel.

CHAPTER XV.

MR. JELLIPOT found, when he reached his office, that Ada Hamilton was waiting to see him.

"I thought you ought to know," she said, "that Inspector Combridge was in the house for over two hours last night. He questioned Mildred—she's the housemaid—an endless time, and gave it up when he found she'd got nothing to say that he could twist round—"

Mr. Jellipot interrupted to say: "I don't think, Miss Hamilton, that that's quite a fair word to use. I've known Inspector Combridge for some time, and my experience is that he wishes to be fair to everyone, and to get at the truth."

"When he's begun by making up his mind what it's going to be? All the questions he asked Mildred were trying to get her to say that she'd seen me poisoning my stepmother, or that I made a point of preparing her food myself, or something suspicious of that kind. He even hinted to Mildred that it must be she or I, and if she wished to clear herself she couldn't do better than think of something to show that I'd done it. You can't expect me to be very pleased about that."

"No. Your resentment was natural. But the inspector, like ourselves, is in a very difficult position. At present, it's a baffling mystery, and it's one that his superior officers are looking to him to solve. But if, as you say, the girl didn't tell him anything of the kind he wanted to get, I don't see that you need trouble about that. Rather the other way."

"Yes. But it didn't end there. When he gave her up, he had a go at the cook, and he got something out of her that he thought important enough to take her off in a taxi, and when she was brought back at midnight, or near enough, she told Mildred she'd promised not to say anything, and now she goes about with her lips twisted up as though she were afraid that they'd blurt it out if she forgot for half a minute to keep them shut."

Mr. Jellipot looked grave at this, but he saw that imagination might easily take them beyond the fact, which might be different from, or even opposite to that which they were disposed to fear.

"There may be very little in it," he said. "Some women of her class are fond of appearing important in such connections, or, if she'd really told him anything, it may be a step toward that solution that we're all trying to get."

"Yes, of course," Ada replied, though with no satisfaction in her voice, "so it may. But, if it were, do you think that the woman would look down whenever she sees me?"

"Do you mean she looks as though she'd done you an injury or as though she is professing to regard you as a probable criminal?"

"She looks like a woman who knows she's done something dirty to the one she doesn't want to look at."

"I see.... What do you think it probable that she may have said?"

"I've no idea; and I don't feel inclined to ask her."

"No. Probably better not. Perhaps I can find out in another way.... But there's a different matter I want to mention. I've made a call on your cousin Vincent this morning, and, in the first place, you may like to know that he is very definitely on your side, if his own assurances are to be credited. He said, with perhaps more emphasis than the opinion required, that the police show a characteristic obtuseness in not recognizing that you are incapable of such a crime. He added that he would willingly come to you at any moment, if he could be of assistance to you."

Miss Hamilton heard this testimonial and offer with a pleasure which she made no effort to conceal.

"I'm glad," she said, "that Vincent takes it like that, though I hoped he would. It's a funny thing that those who aren't over-particular what they do themselves should be more decent in such ways than those who—I expect you know what I mean.

"But there have been times when I've almost wondered whether he hadn't written that card, and I suppose I ought to be a bit ashamed about that myself."

"I don't think," Mr. Jellipot said, "you need blame yourself much for that. It's natural to consider every possibility when you get such a problem, and your cousin isn't one about whom it would be easy to judge what he might or he mightn't do. But it was something else that he said that I think you ought to know, because I have some difficulty in reconciling it with what you told me before.

"He told me that when he used to visit you, a periodical, the name of which, if he recollected rightly, was the *Surgeon-Dentist*, was frequently lying about the house."

"I couldn't agree about that."

"I suppose there is such a paper?"

"Oh, yes. They take it in at the office. But I didn't know that he'd ever seen it, or knew the name."

"Well, it appears that he did. He actually went further than that. He said that he'd seen you reading it more than once. Particularly when he thought that you would have been better occupied in talking to him." Ada Hamilton went white to the lips as she heard this statement; she stared at the solicitor in astonishment or consternation, though which it was Mr. Jellipot found it difficult to decide.

"He really said *that*?" she asked in a tone of real or well-simulated incredulity.

"You mean me to understand that it isn't true?"

"I never read the thing in his presence. Not once in my life. I'm absolutely certain of that. And I'm equally certain that he doesn't think that I did. I suppose that he thought that if he said that it would go a long way to proving that I'd really done it? And you said he was friendly to me?"

"To do him justice—to be merely accurate—I had previously told him that, if you had left such a periodical lying about the house, it might be a point in your favour, rather than otherwise."

She looked partially relieved as she heard this. "You mean," she asked, "that he was making it up because he thought it would do me a good turn?"

"It is a point on which I should not be hasty to form a judgment. For the moment, it is the fact itself on which I am anxious to be sure beyond the possibility of mistake. I am sure you realize the extreme importance, in your own interest, of being exact in the instructions which you give me, and on which I am bound to act."

"Well, I've told you the fact. It's not a matter about which I should be likely to make a mistake! Philip would tell you the same. I believe he did."

"Yes. That was why I was surprised by Mr. Vincent's statement, and wished for your own confirmation or denial."

"You didn't tell him that Philip said differently?"

"No. I was engaged in the collection, not the distribution of information.... But you did quite right to come and tell me about the cook, and I'll follow it up. I suppose it hasn't occurred to you that they may have got some admissions out of her by which the letter-writer can be traced, or even that she's the culprit herself?"

"No. I don't think it has. It wouldn't fit somehow with the way she looked at me in the hall. But of course it might be."

"Well, go home, and don't worry. We seem to be getting on, though it isn't very clear where we shall end."

With these words, Mr. Jellipot shook hands with his client, and sat down silently for a long hour after she had left, and while his morning's business stood still, particularly reviewing his interview with Vincent Hamilton, and endeavouring to penetrate that gentleman's elusive mind.

CHAPTER XVI.

MR. JELLIPOT moved at last. His hand stretched out to the telephone. He said: "Get me Inspector Combridge, if you can." Having said this, he relapsed into his previous impassivity. He felt as a bookkeeper might whose work is blocked by a column of figures which persist in adding to an impossible total. He is tired of the abortive labour of arriving at a figure that he cannot accept. He can observe no error in his own careful casting. He can make no progress in his work until he has overcome this elusive obstacle. Wearily he recommences the unhopeful labour.... A quarter of an hour passed, and the telephone rang, stirring Mr. Jellipot to life again.

"That you, Combridge? Yes, of course it's the Hamilton case. What else do I think of now? I might as well be on vacation, or perhaps better, because the clerks would know then that they'd got to carry on without help from me. I've made some progress—at least I'm not sure that's the right word—but I cannot see where it leads. And I hear you've been at the Hamiltons' cook. I thought we might perhaps proceed on the maxim that exchange is no robbery."

He heard a sound at the other end of the wire which the most sanguine imagination could not construe as that of enthusiastic assent to this proposition. He added: "I've had a talk with Vincent Hamilton. He may have said more than he would to you."

There was a pause of silence, and then he heard: "Shall you be free if I come along now?"

"Yes," he said, "as soon as you like," and turned his mind resolutely to the consideration of the morning's letters that had lain unopened for his attention since he had entered the office.

He had reason to be speedy in what he did, for it was not more than twenty minutes before the inspector was shown in, and his mind must return to the problem which they were equally bent to solve.

"I want," Inspector Combridge began at once, "to trade with you, if I can. If you've got Vincent to talk, which we couldn't do,

I'd give something to know what he said, but I can't see how I'm to give you anything back without doing something else, which I'm quite entitled to do, but which is rather too much like hitting below the belt if you don't understand what the bargain's likely to mean."

"I am not afraid," the solicitor answered, "that you would do that. But it seems to me that I'm offering you a good deal more than I ask, and it's a bargain you ought to be glad to close.

"You've taken a statement from the cook, and you attach sufficient importance to it to tell her to keep her mouth shut, and I've reason to think—you won't ask me to be more explicit—that that statement has some relation to the case you are trying to make against Miss Hamilton.

"If I am wrong on that point, I may have no right to ask for any information as to what the statement contains, but if I am right, then it is a fundamental rule of English judicial practice that accused persons are entitled to know what charges are made against them, so that I am asking no more than I am entitled to know, whereas I am under no obligation of any kind to inform you of what Vincent Hamilton said to me."

"You may be right about that, more or less, if we had taken down a statement which we proposed to put in as evidence, and if we had already arrested Miss Hamilton, and if she had been formally charged.

"But the fact is that, apart from you having raised this question, we didn't intend to arrest her before we had completed the enquiry which you asked us to undertake, about which I can tell you that the firm made no difficulty at all, and we've got two good men now engaged in going over their order files, which show us more than the ledgers would.

"But if I tell you what the cook's statement contains, I may feel it necessary to make the arrest at once."

"I don't see why you should do that."

"To avoid possible tampering with witnesses."

"I must thank you for having told me so frankly. It is a difficulty which our united experiences ought to be able to overcome."

"I'll tell you this. The cook's evidence was mainly hearsay. She didn't admit that she'd seen or heard or done anything herself. But she had been told certain things, and if that be true, and these things actually happened, about which there's not much reasonable doubt, there's a case against Miss Hamilton which you won't find it easy to meet, and which would, we consider, justify an immediate arrest.

"But I wanted to give you every possible opportunity of showing us that there's a different solution—and of course I don't want to make any mistake myself—and so I was willing to wait a few hours while we checked up on the directions in which that drug had been recently sold.

"Now if you've got information from Vincent which bears on the case, and which you don't mind passing on, I recognize that it may possibly be something vital for me to know, and I see that I shouldn't be telling you anything about which, sooner or later, we shouldn't have to turn up the cards.

"But if I tell you now, you can be on the phone the moment I leave, and set Miss Hamilton queering the pitch."

"I'm not sure," Mr. Jellipot smiled, "that you haven't told me enough already to enable me to do that, if I thought it were a desirable course to take. But I'm not sure that it is, and, in any event, I don't want any development leading to an arrest, which I still hope to avoid.

"I ought also to say that you mustn't expect too much from what I got out of Vincent. He talked freely, and what he said has kept my mind busy ever since. But I don't know how much was true, and you might think it quite unimportant whether it's true or not.

"But if we're to tell each other what we've found out, which seems the most sensible thing to do, I'm willing to agree that while you don't make an arrest I'll treat anything you tell me as confidential beyond a point on which we may agree when we've talked it over."

"That's good enough for me. What happened was this. We questioned the housemaid first, and she denied everything, as she'd done before. She said she'd seen and heard nothing suspicious of any kind. It was evident that she was attached to her mistress, and hostile to us. But she gave us the impression that she was telling the truth, all the same. I should say she's a good liar, as such girls often are.

"Then we had another go at the cook, and she took the same line at first, but it wasn't so cleverly done. It was evident that she wasn't comfortable, and at last, with some pressure, it came out. She says that before Mrs. Hamilton died, the housemaid Mildred had remarked to her more than once about the funny way Miss Hamilton had of taking the medicine bottles into a dressing-room, out of the sick woman's sight, and putting something into them."

"Which she used to do when Mildred was looking on?" Mr. Jellipot asked sceptically.

"You know that isn't fair. People are often overseen when it's the last thing that they wish or expect."

"More than once? You spoke of it as a plural occurrence."

"Yes. Perhaps so. If curiosity had been aroused. But I'm not arguing that it's true. I'm telling you the statement we've got, which is very different from what Mildred said. We've got to face the fact that she'll probably be a hostile witness, and deny it, or explain it away if she can. And of course the value of it must depend mainly upon the nature of her own testimony when she's heard what the cook says."

"Well," Mr. Jellipot said cautiously, "I can't take it quite so seriously as you seem to do, especially as it doesn't sound probable in itself, and doesn't come from the one who is alleged to have seen it; but I'll agree with you that it's a point that needs clearing up, which, for the moment, it's understood that I'm not to attempt. I must still hope that you will discover that the drug has been purchased recently in a direction that will put us on the right trail, and that brings me to the interview I had with Vincent this morning."

Mr. Jellipot went on to repeat the conversation which he had had with that gentleman as exactly as a very orderly and retentive memory would allow him to do, and with an impartiality and candour which did not even omit Vincent Hamilton's opinion of the thickness of a detective's skull, on which point he may have reflected that Inspector Combridge's expressed dislike of one whom he regarded as a too-ingenious criminal could not easily be increased.

The inspector was a good listener, and heard the narrative to its conclusion without interruption. Having finished it, Mr. Jellipot said: "I've given it some thought since I came away, but I can't say that I've come to any certainty as to how much to believe. If it isn't asking too much, I wish you'd tell me just how it strikes you."

"Well, I don't mind doing that. I don't see that it gets either of us very far, but it saves time in turning us back from a wrong road.

"I should say it clears Vincent from having written the letter. And though I don't like the man, it's fair to say that, as far as we can check his facts, he seems to have been telling the truth, as, for instance, about his not having been near the house during recent weeks. And where we can't, as about that dentistry paper being always lying about, it sounds a most likely thing; though whether it's a fact that will do Ada Hamilton any good, as you seem to have persuaded him to believe, is a matter on which we should be likely to disagree.

"That's what I think of his facts. When you come to his opinions, it's quite up another street. If he's really a bit in love with Miss Hamilton, it's natural that he should try to persuade himself that she's an innocent woman, and the only importance of that is that it shows he couldn't have written the letter, because he wouldn't have been trying to get her into a mess, let alone knowing what had occurred. But it doesn't alter my opinion about her.

"When he says that it was written by someone in the house, well, I think he's wrong, because there's no one except the cook to suspect, and it isn't her style of work.

"Whether we're really as big as fools as he says, I'm not sure, though I often feel that I am. But, for what a fool's opinion is worth, I think the plain truth is that Ada Hamilton poisoned her stepmother, and every enquiry we make points us the same way, as, if that's the truth, it's quite natural it should."

"And that," Mr. Jellipot said thoughtfully, "is how it appears to you."

"Yes, with one qualification, and that's an idea that only came into my head as you spotted the weakest point in this tale we've had from the cook—Mrs. Miles they call her by the way, though she tells us she isn't married."

"It is the etiquette of her profession, if I am not misinformed."

"Yes, I dare say. But that wasn't what I was trying to say. It didn't sound quite natural, that, if Ada were poisoning the old lady, she should make a habit of doing it with the housemaid looking on, though it might be explained, and it's wonderful how silly the things are that some poisoners do.

"But suppose North had given her the drug to put into the old lady's medicine, and kidded her that it was something to ease pain, or do the heart good, she might have put it into the medicine where the patient couldn't see what she was at, but hardly given a thought to whether anyone else saw her or not."

"Yes," Mr. Jellipot agreed, though still in a preoccupied manner, as being less concerned with the inspector's theories than a train of thought in his own mind, "it doesn't sound likely, but it's another idea, and we can't have too many of them.

"If it were the truth," he added with more animation, "I should be sorry for Ada, because it would be the Bywater's case over again.[2] I mean, they'd hang each other, because no one would know for certain how the guilt lay, and neither could be reprieved without the risk that the less guilty were being hanged; and they couldn't both be reprieved, because it would be too wicked a crime."

---

[2] See *Black Widow*.

Inspector Combridge made no effort to dispute this proposition, and Mr. Jellipot reverted to that which had been on his mind previously.

"You've told me how it strikes you at a first hearing," he said, "and it's only fair that I should tell you how it appeared to me, and of an idea that I can't accept, and that yet I cannot persuade myself to throw altogether aside.

"As I came away from the hotel, I was strongly disposed toward the theory that Vincent had contrived the murder himself, with the purpose of throwing suspicion upon Ada Hamilton, such as, while it might not be strong enough to lead to her arrest, would result in the breaking of her engagement with North, and so clear the way for her marriage to him, after he had earned her gratitude by showing confidence in her, at a time when others would be likely to draw aside."

Mr. Jellipot stated this theory with some hesitation, expecting that the inspector's less visionary mind would dismiss it with the ignominy it deserved. He hastened to add: "But on further reflection I saw that, apart from what you may be disposed to consider its intrinsic improbabilities (which I do not deny), there are particular difficulties which have obliged me to put it definitely aside."

But, surprisingly, he found that the inspector received it with respectful seriousness.

"I don't say," he replied, "that it doesn't sound a bit wild, and it's not the sort of case we should like to put into a brief unless we'd got it worked up a bit better than it stands now.

"But there's one thing in its support that may make it worthwhile to give it a bit more thought before turning it down.

"You know it's said that even the cleverest criminals make the mistake of repeating themselves, so that if they pull off one coup successfully, they don't seem able to resist the temptation to do it over again in such a way that you can recognize who's been at work, and go straight for the right address.

"Now I don't mean that Vincent Hamilton has poisoned anyone before, or even written anonymous letters, though it's more than likely he has done the latter, but if you look at the way he laid his plans for lifting that five hundred pounds out of his landlord's pocket, there are similarities that make it easy to think they might both be the work of the same brain."

"That's very much how I feel about it. I feel he'd be running true to type, and he's the sort of man who could have written the letter, and wouldn't have scrupled to do it. In fact, any theory of the kind sweeps half our difficulties out of the way.

"The trouble is that it brings others up which are even bigger than those that we're fighting now. If it had been no more than a hoax, by which Ada was to fall under suspicion, so that Philip would be likely to throw her over, while Vincent showed himself the true friend till the cloud had cleared, it would be likely enough But there's the fact that we're dealing with a real murder, and Vincent wouldn't contrive that merely for the sake of raising a suspicion that he might find it much harder to clear away.

"I have been telling myself that for the last hour, but it is a most remarkable thing that the idea persists, with an illogical feeling that it would get me home if I could only follow it up in the right way."

"That," Inspector Combridge answered with confidence, "must be because it's what you want to believe. It would get your client clear, and might start Vincent on his way to the cells, where there's no doubt that he ought to be. But, as you say, it won't fit the facts, and when they won't do that it's about the hardest lesson we have to learn that theories have got to go."

"It is the counsel of common sense," Mr. Jellipot agreed, though still looking rather as though he were being reluctantly forced to admit that one of his own children was unfit to live, and that the death-warrant must be countersigned by his own hand. He became precise in definition of the bargain that they had made: "It is agreed that I shall say nothing to Miss Hamilton, or to her household staff, and perhaps I should add to anyone by whom communication might be made to any of them, concerning the allegations that Mrs. Miles has made; and, on your part, that you will not proceed to the extremity of the arrest of my client before the scrutiny of the manufacturers' order file has been completed. May I ask, even if that investigation should be negative in its result, that we may still meet for a final discussion of the position; and in case I should then be better placed to demonstrate my client's innocence than I now am, before the actual issuing of the warrant against her?"

"Yes, I don't mind promising that. I'm always ready to listen to anything you can say, and I don't pretend that the case, even with the cook's tale thrown into the scale, is as complete as we should like it to be.... That's, of course, if she doesn't try doing a bolt, or he either. I don't suppose I need tell you that we've not let either out of our sight since the coroner's court was adjourned."

"If 'he' means Philip North, it was a guess which would not have been hard to make. But I don't think there'll be any attempt at running away."

Mr. Jellipot pulled out his watch as he spoke, and was amazed to see that the hands stood at 2:55 P.M. He said: "I don't suppose

93

you've had lunch, any more than I. How about going round the corner together?"

But the inspector said that he had to be back at the Yard for an
appointment at 2:45, and hurried away.

CHAPTER XVII.

INSPECTOR COMBRIDGE was going through Mr. Jellipot's outer door when he met Ada Hamilton too directly to avoid the hand which she held out to him in a formal greeting, though there was angry hostility in her eyes, and in the tone with which she spoke: "Don't you think, Inspector, that it would have been straighter to tell me what Mrs. Miles said? You might have saved yourself a good deal of trouble."

Used as he was to encounter difficult positions, he was momentarily taken aback by this unexpected onslaught: "In such matters, Miss Hamilton, you must allow us to use our own discretion," he said awkwardly.

"Discretion?" she echoed, with more spirit than he had seen her show previously. "Are you sure that's the right word? Well, don't ask *me* now. Ask Dr. Burfoot what I was instructed to do."

She went through the door without giving time for a reply, and he descended the lift feeling more disconcerted than his reason told him that the occasion required, and with a thought that Mr. Jellipot's lunch seemed likely to be further delayed.

"I'm sorry," Ada said, as she met the solicitor in turn coming out of his inner door. "I didn't mean to worry you again today, but I found when I reached home that Mildred had got it out of the cook, without my having to ask, and I thought it was something you ought to know."

It was a position which had not been anticipated in the bargain of silence which Mr. Jellipot had so recently made, but he observed it with a scrupulous literality, as he said: "You did quite rightly to come at once. You'd better sit down and tell me what the woman said."

"She said that Mildred had seen me putting things into Mrs. Hamilton's medicine."

"That was a serious allegation to make. What does Mildred say?"

"She says she meant no harm, as of course she didn't, when she mentioned it to the cook. It was just idle talk, while my stepmother was still alive, and no one had any idea about poisoning in their heads. But she says she didn't mention it to the police, because she felt sure they'd twist it round the wrong way.

"She didn't even think that the cook would remember anything that she'd said, it being just casual talk at the time."

"But do you mean that it was true?"

"Of course it was, or Mildred wouldn't have been likely to say she saw it. I used to put water in the medicine at times on Dr. Burfoot's instructions, because my stepmother would take double doses to ease the pain, although Dr. Burfoot had told her it was a dangerous thing to do. I usually left a dose of the right strength for her to have during the night, but if she wouldn't accept that, and wanted the bottle left, Dr. Burfoot had told me to dilute it sufficiently to make sure that what was left didn't amount to a dangerous quantity. It meant pouring some away once, and, when I reminded her, Mildred remembers that she may have seen me doing that too.

"But she didn't see me do anything except that, about which I'm sure that Dr. Burfoot will bear me out that it was what he'd told me to do."

"Very well. I'm glad you've told me of this. I will let Inspector Combridge know about it at the right time, and meanwhile you can put it out of your mind."

He was standing while this conversation took place, with his hat in his hand, and, seeing that he was prepared to go out, Miss Hamilton had discretion enough not to delay him with further detail.

Not knowing of her conversation with Inspector Combridge, he took some satisfaction in imagining an interview with that gentleman at which the threat that she could no longer remain at liberty would be met by the devastating simplicity of this explanation.

But he did not blind himself to the fact that though the case for Ada's prosecution might seem incomplete while no one could say that they had seen her administer the poison, or could trace it definitely to her possession, and while the writer of the anonymous letter could not be identified (for if there be an elusive letter-writer, why not an elusive murderer also?), yet this incompleteness of the case against her was no more evident than was the weakness of her own position while it remained an unchallenged fact that Mrs. Hamilton had died from this obscure poison, and no one but herself could be suggested with motive and opportunity to commit the crime.

Of course, if she had been in league with Dr. Burfoot, if he had connived at, or even instigated the crime, that would account for her relying upon him to support an explanation which no one else could deny. He, at least, had had opportunity. He might have done it entirely himself! But why should he?

For the time, Mr. Jellipot gave it up....

He turned his attention to other business matters of pressing importance during the afternoon and the following morning, thinking that it might be better to defer further consideration of a baffling problem until Inspector Combridge should communicate the substance of the wholesalers' report, concerning which he had some hope, though not much.

And meanwhile Inspector Combridge was a harassed man.

In the first place, the Assistant-commissioner had asked for a full report of the Hamilton case to be on his desk within twenty-four hours, and this sudden interest in its position was understood to be the result of an anonymous letter he had received by the morning post, the contents of which he had not divulged; so that the inspector must present his facts and deductions without knowing what disclosures might be in Sir Henry Cotham's possession, which is not a pleasant position for an officer who has a reputation to sustain; and must now either admit that he is floundering in a bog of doubt while the simple solution may already be in Sir Henry's hands, or make a show of wisdom, which may prove to be no better than incompetence when its conclusions are contrasted with that same solution.

Apart from this, he had seen Dr. Burfoot, who had said that he had had no communication from Miss Hamilton, but when asked whether he could give any explanation of the incidents that Mildred was alleged to have seen, he replied at once that they were quite probably no more than the result of his own instructions.

He said that the medicine he had prescribed for Mrs. Hamilton required an exact dosage, concerning which his patient had been difficult. She was a woman of sudden impulses, and impatient of pain, and after she had once been seriously affected by an overdose she had taken, he had arranged with Miss Hamilton that she should take such precautions as might appear necessary at any time to prevent a repetition of the incident.

Inspector Combridge saw here not merely the loss of evidence which had seemed to him a few hours before sufficient to justify recommending an arrest, he saw also a pit of trouble into which he had almost slipped would, indeed, have slipped beyond doubt, but for Ada Hamilton's angry words, which shrewder advice might have warned her to leave unspoken.

For such an accusation, made in open court, and then disproved, would not leave the case where it was, as though it had not been made. It would, however illogically, alienate the sympathies of an average jury, so that a verdict, which might otherwise have been certain, might be very hard to obtain.

After what Dr. Burfoot had said, he knew that he must utterly abandon that line of attack, unless he were to discredit the doctor himself, which he had no reason to suppose that he would be able to do.

He saw also that this evidence was in Ada's favour in another, though it might be less than a conclusive, direction.

Under the circumstances of which Dr. Burfoot had spoken, how easily might she have given a dangerous overdose to the patient in her charge, if she had wished her death, rather than take the risk of a rare drug, the action of which she could not gauge with accuracy either from her own experience or the published reports of its use as an anæsthetic in smaller quantities.

And, further than this, did not Dr. Burfoot's statement tend to suggest that it might, after all, be a case of self-destruction deliberately intended, or the result of a secret experiment with a drug by which she thought to relieve her pain?

This last idea took serious hold of his mind, till he came to doubt whether a crime had been committed at all. But for the fact of the anonymous letters, of the contents of the second of which he was so maddeningly ignorant, he would have been tempted to make a report emphasizing the possibility that the poison had been self-administered, but whether with, or without, intention of suicide there was insufficient evidence to decide.

But he saw that Sir Henry Cotham would be unlikely to regard it as a case which could be properly closed while the source of those letters was undiscovered, and the suggested explanation was itself no more than a plausible possibility, unless he could show a means by which Mrs. Hamilton could have secured a supply of the fatal drug.

This consideration led him to the examination of the report of its recent sales, which was now before him.

It appeared that, during the three months that it had been on the market, 503 orders had been executed, of which 136 were in the area of Greater London. All of these had been supplied to hospitals, dentists, doctors, licensed vivisectors, and one veterinary surgeon. The customers' names had been tabulated in alphabetical order, and that of Dr. Burfoot was not among them.

The evidence was therefore of a negative character. It did not exclude the possibility that the drug might have found its way to Mrs. Hamilton's bedroom by some other channel than that of the

Corbin Street dental-surgery—the total number of people who could have had access to those 136 supplies must be large. To prove a negative is proverbially difficult. But an examination of the list appeared to Inspector Combridge to make it immensely more probable that Ada Hamilton had procured the drug, either with or without Philip North's assistance, and the idea of suicide or any other form of self-administration receded proportionately.

His mind hardened again in its inclination to draw up the report in such a way as to indicate Ada Hamilton as the certain criminal, with Philip North as a probable confederate, and to assert that he was already in possession of information almost sufficient to justify an arrest, which he expected to complete at an early date.

His greatest difficulty in adopting that position was that the expectation which he must assert was far from being of a confident kind. If Sir Henry should say: "Yes, that seems quite satisfactory. What is the next step that you are proposing to take?" his reply might not be easy to frame; but even on this point he could find some confidence in memories of previous cases which had had their moments of apparent deadlock, but over which his pertinacity had finally triumphed.

And even now there was a development, however limited in its probable significance, in the reports of the excellent officers who had been selected to keep observation upon the two who were under greatest suspicion. From the moment when the inquest had been adjourned, both Ada Hamilton and Philip North had been continually shadowed, with the double object of ensuring that they should not escape, and of observing any suspicious circumstance in their behaviour. Last night, the two officers had found that their duties had become one, for the two people that they had been separately following had met in a Richmond tea-room, and then taken a boat on the river, during which time it had only been possible to observe them from the bank. Their demeanour during the time, the reports agreed, had been fairly friendly, but, in the quaint phrasing of Detective Jenkins, "without demonstrations of sexual familiarity."

In fact, they had appeared while in the boat to have been engaged in an earnest conversation, which had become at times, to quote from Detective Jenkins again, "of a disputatious rather than a quarrelsome character." During that time, their words could not be overheard. Only gestures could be observed. But when they landed from the boat, and Detective Jenkins was reluctantly keeping some distance away, it having been agreed between himself and his comrade that it would be imprudent for them both to follow too closely, the conversation between the lovers, or murderers, or whatever we may conclude them to have been, had continued with animation, and Detective Eales, a mere five yards behind in the Kew Road, had heard enough to conclude that the dentist had been urging his female companion to some course of conduct which she was afraid or reluctant to take.

Their voices had been regrettably low, and Detective Eales, a conscientious man with two sisters in the Salvation Army, was too scrupulous to commit himself to words of which he was less than sure, but he had distinctly heard Miss Hamilton say (and had noted down at the first available moment), "It's no use saying that! It would make it look worse than it does now"; while the names of Mr. Jellipot and Inspector Combridge himself (disrespectfully alluded to by Mr. North as "that prying Swine") had been audible at times, and appeared to indicate the subject on which they talked.

"They always," Inspector Combridge, speaking from a long experience, said to himself as he read this—"they always hang themselves if you give them enough rope. I wonder what fool thing they're thinking of doing now?"

He felt in better spirits after considering these reports, but the idea of Ada Hamilton's immediate arrest, which had been his programme of yesterday if the manufacturers' report should be as negative as it had proved, had faded out with the collapse of Mrs. Miles's evidence, and the Assistant-Commissioner's requisition. It did not therefore occur to him that there was urgent occasion for communicating with Mr. Jellipot, and he might have delayed the passing on of the manufacturers' report till the following morning, while he wrestled with the more urgent problem of the report, but he had drafted no more than three abortive commencements, when he was disturbed by Sergeant Belfrey's voice on the telephone: "It's Mr. Jellipot, sir. Shall I put him through?"

CHAPTER XVIII.

"I WONDERED," Mr. Jellipot's voice enquired, "whether you could let me know—of course in the strictest confidence—whether any gambling dens are to be raided tonight?"

Mr. Jellipot was a solicitor in extensive practice, but to Inspector Combridge, in his present mood, he existed only as a factor in the Hamilton case. The question, unusual in itself, was therefore particularly unexpected. "I'm afraid," he said, "I don't understand."

"It seems," Mr. Jellipot replied, with a nervous asperity, "a simple question to me."

"It isn't one I could answer, anyway. I'm likely enough to have to send in my resignation without that."

"You will not suppose," Mr. Jellipot replied coldly, "that I should ask such a question against the interests of the law."

"No, I don't suppose you would. But regulations exist, all the same. Do you mind telling me why you want to know?"

"I have had an invitation to visit one at twelve-thirty tonight."

"Tell me the name now, and I'll see whether we can't spare a squad to raid it at twelve-fifteen."

"I don't know the name, and I'm not asking you to raid anywhere."

"Well, when you count your money tomorrow morning, you'll wish we had. Let me know when you're stopping the cheque. It's almost always a justifiable thing to do."

"I can assure you," Mr. Jellipot replied, with simple seriousness, "that I shall not lose."

"No? Well, I'm told that they let the mugs win the first night. But if they think you'll have too much sense to return, they clear you out while they've got the chance.... But if you know you'll win, what do you want me to do? Send an escort when you're getting the winnings home?"

"I wished," Mr. Jellipot explained, in a voice the seriousness of which contrasted with the inspector's flippancy, "to avoid the possibility of my name being taken in a raid, or of the contingency that I might even be detained if it were not understood that I shall be there in a strictly professional capacity. It is a kind of publicity which I should particularly dislike to have."

"Oh, you needn't mind about that. The last raid we had we hauled in a permanent undersecretary and two barristers and a Fleet Street peer.... But if you're serious, hold on a moment."

Inspector Combridge, having made some enquiries on another wire, concluded the conversation with: "I'm not answering the question you asked, nor promising anything, but I don't see that you need worry more than a bit."

"Thank you," Mr. Jellipot replied with his usual placidity. "I felt sure that you would be able to let me know."

He spoke as though he were closing the conversation, and the inspector remembered that he was under a promise to inform him of the contents of the report that was on his desk. He said: "Oh, by the way, I've got particulars now of all the sales of the drug that have been made from when it was first put on the market about three months ago. They're all to hospitals and practitioners and those you'd expect to order. I'm afraid they won't help you at all."

"But you're not going to arrest Miss Hamilton all the same?"

There was a quiet confidence in the solicitor's voice which the inspector disliked, and the source of which he felt that it was easy to guess. "I suppose," he said, "the girls' been telling you that there's an explanation of the cook's tale?"

"She did mention the incident to me. She appeared to think that the impetuosity of the police sometimes outruns their discretion. It is a point of view which the occurrence in question is inconclusive to support, but I was precluded from much which I might have put forward in your defence by the pledge of silence which you had asked me to give.

"But, if you will excuse the pertinacity of the legal mind, you have not answered the question I asked."

"I don't suppose that, apart from some unexpected development, anything will be decided today."

"I think the delay may be wise. I am hopeful of being able to discover something myself during the next day or two."

"Well, so are we."

"Though," Mr. Jellipot added cautiously, "I have no grounds for that expectation such as I could set out in a logically convincing statement. You might call it an intuition."

"Well, I don't mind doing that. I've had them myself before now. They're most often wrong."

Inspector Combridge put back the receiver, and went on with his interrupted report.

But a few moments later he resorted to the telephone again. He gave instructions that a capable man was to follow Mr. Jellipot from when he left his office until he should arrive at his own home, however late that might be. If, as was most probable, he should visit one of the gambling hells of Soho or Bayswater, the man must remain until he should come out, and must take particular notice of anyone who might enter or leave with him. Should he part from such a companion, that man rather than Mr. Jellipot must be followed, and his identity established.

He was late in completing the report, and late consequently in arriving at Scotland Yard next morning, and when he did so he found that Detective Solomon was waiting to see him.

Detective-Sergeant Solomon was one of the best of the alert and resourceful officers who specialize in the suppression of the illegal night-clubs and gambling dens that break out continually in the West End of London, like the pimples of an eruptive fever, so that those who make war upon them have a work that is never done.

He was an officer usually engaged in organizing rather than executing the sudden raids by which these places are brought under the penalties of the law, as the fact that he was sometimes used to penetrate them in disguise, and so obtain the information by which raids could be timed successfully, rendered it undesirable that his face should become familiar to those he hunted.

He was a dark-skinned, dark-eyed Jew, with black hair, oiled and waved, who needed little get-up to present him as a natural habitué of such resorts. He had now an expression of dissatisfaction for which there was some excuse, his zeal for the service having led him to lose a night's rest in a monotonous vigil which he might have delegated to a subordinate had he foreseen how unimportant his observations were destined to be.

"I am afraid, sir," he said, "I have not much to report. I kept Mr. Jellipot under observation, as your instructions were. He left his office at 6:13 P.M. and he went straight home—"

"I hope you didn't leave him at that?" Inspector Combridge exclaimed, realizing with some deserved self-criticism that a literal obedience to his instructions would have allowed him to do so.

"Naturally not, sir. I waited till 11:45 P.M. when he came out and walked to the end of the road in Wimbledon where he lives, and caught the last bus to town. He got off at Piccadilly Circus, and walked to the top of Albemarle Street, where he waited a short time until a taxi drew up to the pavement, and a gentleman inside opened the door for him to enter.

"They went off round the corner at once at a good pace, the streets being clear at that hour, and I lost them for a moment before I could get another taxi to follow, but I'd made a note of the number, and picked them up again rather luckily. They got out at the Cactus Club."

Inspector Combridge looked surprised, and Solomon answered his unspoken thought. "Yes, sir. So was I. I waited there till 3:35 A.M., when the two gentlemen came out together, but separated at once, taking different taxis.

"I followed Mr. Jellipot's companion, which I understood you'd prefer me to do under such circumstances. He returned to the Raleigh Hotel. I ascertained that his name is Mr. Vincent Hamilton. He's been staying there for some days."

"It wasn't quite what you expected?"

"No, sir. I can't say it was."

"You thought you were being put on the track of a gambling hell that we might have had the pleasure of raiding another night?"

"Yes, sir. There was something said about you having got on the scent of something of the kind. I didn't know that it was anything to do with the Vincent Hamilton matter."

"Nor did I. Nor, for that matter, is it. That case is closed. It may be something to do with the Hamilton murder case. I don't know yet. But I can understand that you didn't expect to end up at the Cactus Club. Notice anyone else specially going in there?"

"No, sir. There were just about the usual lot. Lady Cleve took a party in."

"Well, thanks. You've found out all I wanted to know."

Sergeant Solomon went, and Inspector Combridge digested the information he had received. His mind was half puzzled, half amused, and alertly aware of the possibility—indeed, the certainty—that he was on the threshold of something unexpected, and of potential importance.

The Cactus was a night-club certainly. It might be said that it was *the* night-club. But it was not one which the police would be likely to raid. It was certainly not a gambling hell! And Jellipot had been nervous as to whether he would be disgraced if he were caught in a raid! Why, it was a club to which the Assistant-Commissioner himself would sometimes go with his wife, who had been Lottie Leland before her marriage, and would not allow the world to forget that she could still dance, though she might be the mother of twins. The Prime Minister had been seen there less than two months ago.

Foreign diplomats would resort there, feeling that their discretion could not be impugned, that their dignity would be unimpaired. The Cactus was a night-club, indeed. It was one of worldwide repute. But that there are night-clubs *and* night-clubs was evidently a fact of which Mr. Jellipot was too innocent to be aware. The inspector smiled at the elderly solicitor's ignorance of the night-life of his native city.

But, to be fair, Jellipot had said that he had not known where he was to be taken. Hearing this, it had been a friendly precaution for his own safety, as well as curiosity to discover where he would be led, which had inclined the inspector to have him followed.

And he had been taken there by Vincent Hamilton!—a man who, it might reasonably be supposed, would be himself unable to enter the lordly doors, either as member or member's friend.

There was almost certainly some trickery here, some subtle game that Vincent Hamilton had in hand for Mr. Jellipot's undoing. Yet the solicitor, in his own way, was both cautious and shrewd. He might be equal to his own protection. But Inspector Combridge felt less than sure. Vincent Hamilton had been too much for himself. It would have required an unusual modesty to regard it as certain that he would not outwit Mr. Jellipot also.

Yet Inspector Combridge felt vaguely pleased. He felt like a watching cat that sees the mouse move a few inches out of its hole. It is still beyond reach, but there is hope in the evident fact that it is disposed to emerge again. Whatever part (if any) Vincent Hamilton might have had in the writing of the anonymous letter, or Mrs. Hamilton's murder, it had seemed impossible to prove anything against him while he remained quiet, but if he should become active in some new duplicity in which Mr. Jellipot was to be involved, well, one thing leads to another. And how often before had Inspector Combridge watched criminals manufacturing evidence for their own doom, while they thought that they were making additionally sure of their own immunity!

What, he wondered, had happened during the night? As to that, he could, at least, have Mr. Jellipot's version. After the conversation of the previous afternoon some enquiry was natural, and a reply could hardly, in courtesy, be refused. He rang to the operator to get him through to Mr. Jellipot as quickly as possible, and soon heard the solicitor's voice at the other end of the wire.

"You don't," he answered Mr. Jellipot's polite good-morning, "sound as though you're much the worse for your night out."

"No, I can't say that I am. Perhaps those of us who are of regular and abstemious habits may be better able to sustain an occasional dissipation, that being a word which I cannot entirely repudiate as a description of my nocturnal experiences, than are those who indulge with greater frequency in such foolish and untimely enterprises."

"Pleased to hear it," the inspector replied; "I shouldn't wonder if you're quite right." And then, not having been acutely interested in this abstract speculation, he resumed his own enquiry: "Was it as low a den as you had expected to find?"

"No, it would not be fair to say that. There were evidences of extravagance and the misuse of wealth which I was sorry, but less surprised, to observe."

"Quite a lot of gambling, I suppose?"

"Yes. In that aspect it was an interesting experience, although not one in which I should prefer to indulge habitually, both from personal and public considerations."

Inspector Combridge was surprised. This was a form and degree of duplicity of which he had not thought Mr. Jellipot capable. How far on the path of inexplicable mendacity would he go?

"Didn't lose much, I hope?" he said in a voice which he tried to make appropriate to the enquiry.

"Oh, no," the reply came, with an accent of slight surprise. "I told you it had been understood that I shouldn't lose. I won the amount—almost exactly the amount—that I had been led to expect."

"You don't mind telling me where the interesting experience occurred?"

"I shouldn't mind at all, but I'm under a promise not to disclose it; and in any case it would require very grave consideration as to whether it would be an honourable course to adopt, in view of the natural difficulty which you would experience in differentiating between your private and official capacities."

"And if I tell you I know already?"

There was a moment's silence, after which Mr. Jellipot said, with his usual placidity: "In that event it would appear reasonable to observe the fact that you could have no occasion to ask."

Inspector Combridge was reduced to a pause of indecision by this reply. He remained silent for a moment, with the receiver still in his hand. Should he say that he knew where Mr. Jellipot had been, and that this talk of a gambling hell was no more than a baseless myth—a deception unworthy of Mr. Jellipot's reputation, or of the confidence which had previously existed between them? Yet what, beyond a possible quarrel, was to be gained? And was his assurance so absolute? Could Solomon have been deceived? Had he followed the wrong men?

So he hesitated, and as he was commencing to speak again, he heard the clink of the disconnection, as Mr. Jellipot, taking the conversation to be concluded, hung up at his end.

Inspector Combridge, feeling that termination might be preferable to further words until he showed himself to be more surely informed, summoned Solomon again. He questioned him closely concerning the following of Mr. Jellipot, and, in particular, respecting the time when he had lost sight of the taxi into which the two men had entered. But Sergeant Solomon had no doubt. He would stake his reputation upon having observed correctly the number of the taxi that he pursued, and of it having been Mr. Jellipot who had come out of the Cactus Club in the early hour of the morning, with Vincent Hamilton at his side.

The inspector knew him to be a man unlikely to deceive himself on such a point, or to make a report of which he was not sure. Besides, if it were not Mr. Jellipot, what an amazing improbability would it be that the second man to be followed should prove to be Vincent Hamilton!

"Very well," he said, "if you're sure. I've no doubt you're right.... By the way, there's no gambling at the Cactus, is there?"

Sergeant Solomon looked doubtful. "There's the card-room, sir. They don't reckon to play for stakes, but I wouldn't like to say that they never do."

"Nor I. But there are no gambling-tables? No roulette-wheels? No baccarat? You know what mean."

"Oh, no, sir. There's never been anything like that there."

"There couldn't be without our knowing?"

"No, sir. I don't see how there could. There are too many go there who wouldn't stand for it. Why, Sir Henry himself drops in sometimes."

CHAPTER XIX.

MR. JELLIPOT would have repudiated with a just indignation the idea that he could have allowed himself to be influenced by anything but consideration for his client's interests in the course he adopted in regard to the writ which had been issued by Mr. Wall's solicitors.

He considered that Vincent Hamilton had no possible legal defence, and that a summons for judgment (the speediest method of disposing of a claim which is beyond any reply to which the most skilful drafter of affidavits can give an appearance of verisimilitude) could have only one possible termination. There would be judgment against his client for £500, with a substantial addition of costs, a proportion of which a prompt settlement might avoid.

He cannot therefore have been acting otherwise than in Vincent Hamilton's interests when he rang up the plaintiff's solicitors and asked them, without prejudice, whether they would be prepared to advise Mr. Wall to allow an extended time for payment, if his own client would consent to immediate judgment. Nor was it open to reasonable criticism that, when he had obtained an affirmative answer, he should have rung Vincent Hamilton up, and asked him to give him a call any time before 4:00 P.M. if he could conveniently do so.

Yet it remains a fact that the law allowed him a period of eight days from the service of the writ (of which five remained) before he was obliged even to enter the appearance which is the formal prelude to litigation in the higher courts, and it is possible to doubt whether he would have felt it necessary to handle the case with such celerity had he not been anxious to have a further talk on the quite separate subject of Mrs. Hamilton's end, and for it to occur in a casual manner.

However this may have been, Mr. Jellipot was certainly conscious of a greater degree of satisfaction when Mr. Hamilton replied readily that he had nothing on for the afternoon, and would look in at two-thirty, than was always aroused by the approaching visit of an uncongenial client, from whom he expected to make no more than an unimportant profit.

Mr. Hamilton arrived punctually. He strolled in with the leisured manner of those who are not harnessed to the routines of industrial or commercial toil. Had he been of an introspective or analytic habit of mind, he might have considered that this freedom of thought and movement, which is possible only to those who inherit wealth, or who prey deliberately upon the industry of their fellows, was not bought too dearly at the price of coldness or even hostility from the classes which supplied his victims, and a constant wariness to outwit the police whom they had prudently established for their own protection.

He came in jauntily, being in good temper both with himself and the world, and having had his mind pleasantly though as yet nebulously occupied upon one of those complicated manoeuvres by which his own pocket became full, without the repellent necessity for personal toil, or the interposition of an unfriendly law. He had his object clearly in view, but the methods by which it should be attained were not rigidly planned. He had no more as yet than a vague design, such as would be watchful to mould fluidity of circumstance to the ultimate purpose he had in view. He had not yet fully decided the part which Mr. Jellipot was to take in the development which he designed, but he saw that he might be useful in several ways, and the solicitor's wish to see him was no greater than the alacrity with which he came.

"It is this matter of Wall *versus* Yourself," Mr. Jellipot began, as soon as he had shaken hands with his client, and seen him sink comfortably into the depths of the padded chair, "on which I am now prepared to take your instructions.

"I am happy to be able to tell you that I have succeeded in persuading the plaintiff's solicitors to advise their client to accept payment by a series of monthly instalments—the actual amount was not agreed, as I indicated that it would be premature until I had ascertained with precision what you would be able to do—but it was understood that it would be a quite moderate figure—a modest figure was the actual word which I felt appropriate to the occasion—and I finally undertook to make them a definite offer—of course, without prejudice—by noon tomorrow."

"You're a quick worker," Mr. Hamilton remarked. "I didn't know there'd be such a rush."

"It is a position in which it appeared to me that nothing would be gained by delay—indeed, quite the reverse—if I should find the plaintiff's solicitors in the mood to accept an offer."

"Well, I'm trusting to you. What do you think they'll be hoping to get now?"

"There was a tentative suggestion of fifty pounds down, and twenty-five pounds monthly, to which I did not respond."

"They'd like to see it, no doubt! I've got no money to throw away now. What's the lowest you think they'd take?"

"It is impossible to say that in advance of an offer being put forward. I am prepared to propose as little as ten pounds down and monthly instalments of the same amounts, if that should be the best which you would feel able to do."

"Why not try eight?"

"I should be disposed to advise the amount I have mentioned, if you wish to reach a settlement."

"And what if I miss paying it now and then?"

"I am afraid it would be a condition that judgment would be signed against you for the full amount, with an undertaking that it would not be enforced so long as the instalments were kept up."

"They'd want a tenner at once?"

"I should prefer to have the first instalment in hand when putting the proposal before them. It might be a material point in offering so moderate an amount to be able to say that I was prepared to pay it on their acceptance being received."

Mr. Hamilton hesitated. He did not wish to appear unappreciative of Mr. Jellipot's efforts on his behalf, and he was aware that, if certain events should develop as he not only hoped but was expecting them to do, it might be a real advantage to him to have this claim fixed in such a way that he could not be pressed for a settlement so long as the instalments were paid. But he hated parting with money for which he saw no return. To pay back anything of this sum which he had schemed to obtain was a necessity he would only reluctantly face whether he had the money or not. It gave him a sense of defeat, and that no less because he was at the moment in ample funds.

Yet the first instalment would be £10 only, and in a month's time he might be better able to see whether he should continue to pay, or tell the hotel proprietor to go to the nether regions.

The result of these reflections was that he said: "Well, you've got five pounds in hand. I might double that if I'm fairly lucky tonight. I can't say that I've got it now."

Mr. Jellipot was particularly anxious not to fall out with his disreputable client, but there was a mild resentment in his reply: "I understood you to say that the five pounds already paid was for the costs which would be incurred, and you may have observed that the receipt I sent you was made out in that way."

"Well, it's a question of how I get on tonight. You can't ask me to pay what I haven't got." He looked at the solicitor as though a new idea had entered his mind. "It might do you no harm if you came along."

It was an invitation which Mr. Jellipot had not expected, and did not understand. Under other circumstances he would have dismissed the suggestion of spending his evening with Vincent Hamilton, whether client or not, as outside serious consideration. But now his expression was such as to give Vincent some encouragement in developing his idea.

"If I should come where?" Mr. Jellipot asked.

"If you should come with me to the club. You could have a try yourself, if you like. I don't touch the baccarat table myself. If you sit down there, it's at your own risk. But they've got *rouge-et-noir* and roulette. You can make a few pounds on them, if you follow me. You'll lose it if you stake too high."

"You are inviting me, as I understand," Mr. Jellipot replied, with his usual precision, "to accompany you tonight to a gambling club, such as must be carried on in this city under fear of the penalty of the law, and you are informing me that the play is of such a character that it is possible to know beforehand when I should fail, or where you can promise that I should win."

"Oh, you mustn't think it's so bad! They couldn't run those places on two percent, and that's all they'd get from the wheel if they let it run loose, without knowing where it would stop."

"That," Mr. Jellipot agreed, "may be quite true, and may explain why those who make a habit of frequenting these games of chance (which you would tell me should be called by another name) may be expected to lose. But it does not tell me how you can promise me in advance that I can win a moderate amount."

Mr. Vincent Hamilton sat with outstretched legs, and for a long moment he looked silently at his boots. He was uncertain whether he had said too much already, or should be still franker in explanation. Mr. Jellipot, who knew the virtue of silence, waited patiently till he asked: "If you're my lawyer, I suppose anything I say doesn't go through the door?"

"With some obvious reservations which it should not be necessary for me to state, a client's confidences must be respected."

"Well, it's like this," Mr. Hamilton began, and explained, with a graphic bluntness, the nature of the appointment he held, withholding only the name of the establishment that retained his services. He pointed out that if Mr. Jellipot did not stake highly enough to annoy the banker, and followed his lead, there was no reason that he should not have the pleasurable experience of a night at the gaming-tables with the exceptional advantage of knowing that when he went to bed he would not be a poorer man.

Mr. Jellipot considered this curious proposition with some reluctance to admit the attraction which it contained. He was not destitute of the adventurous temperament, although his adventures hitherto had been less of the body than of the mind.

On the moral issue, he observed, with some mental subtlety, that he would be wronging no one by putting some moderate stakes on the numbers chosen by Mr. Hamilton, for though the spinner of the wheel might be deliberately cheating the gamblers there, his own action would do nothing to the encouragement of that dishonesty. Rather, the presence of his stake in addition to that of his client, might incline the wheel to be spun to a different purpose, in which event some people might be allowed to win who would have been cheated had he not been there. Neither could it be said that he would be betting on a certainty himself (on the moral obliquity of which he was less than clear, and which he felt he must resolve at a time of greater mental leisure than he had now), for he had no more than the doubtful value of Vincent Hamilton's word for the condition on which he was to rely for success, upon a board which, on the same testimony, was unfairly run.

Putting the moral issue aside, that of expediency remained. But on this point he reminded himself that it had been his first object at this interview to draw Vincent Hamilton into further and more intimate conversation upon the mystery which he could not otherwise solve. Surely therefore the opportunities of intimacy and obligation which were tendered so unexpectedly to him were not lightly to be put aside.

As to the risk of financial loss, he was inclined to think, with some confidence, that his client would not deceive him in such a matter, and in any case, he could limit his risk by taking only a moderate amount of money with him. He thought he knew himself well enough to be assured that he would not plunge beyond that which his wallet held. He asked: "What amounts could I safely stake without risk of loss?"

"You might follow my stakes and let yourself win ten pounds during the night. I shouldn't go beyond that."

"If I bring twenty pounds with me?"

"Yes. I shouldn't bring more than that. I don't want you to plunge, and then blame it on to me."

This being agreed, Mr. Hamilton got up to go, after obtaining a promise that the gambling activities of the club would not be disclosed to anyone without his consent, and in particular not to the Metropolitan police; and fixing the appointment in Albemarle Street which Mr. Jellipot subsequently kept.

Mr. Jellipot would have liked to detain him for the conversation he had in mind, but he said he had another appointment to keep, and the solicitor's discretion led him to decide to wait for the chance of a later hour.

Mr. Hamilton went, and Mr. Jellipot, having given the matter some further thought, was disturbed by the possibility that he might be caught in a police raid, in which event he had a vague impression that he would be locked in the cells during the night, and fined or cautioned in the morning as he would stand in a dock crowded with the hawks and pigeons by whom such resorts (he believed) were peopled. That might not greatly matter; but it might matter much if his name appeared in the Press among a list of such convicted persons; and being disturbed by this thought, he had telephoned Inspector Combridge, with a result which has been recorded already, and which gave him so much assurance that he forthwith required the cashier to hand him twenty pounds from the safe (which was not to be debited to him till the morning, as it would most probably be returned), and resolved to keep the appointment that had been made.

CHAPTER XX.

MR. JELLIPOT was surprised when he entered the Cactus Club. There was some reason for that, but one of more experience of the night resorts of great cities would have been surprised from a different cause.

Mr. Hamilton led him through rooms in which no gambling could be observed, and of a quality which no other night-club could have presumed to rival. Wishing to set him at ease regarding the associations to which he had been brought, he pointed out men and women politically prominent, or of good social repute, who were seated at the tables or dancing to the music of an excellent band. Mr. Jellipot was mildly surprised at the luxury and order of what he saw. He was surprised to be told that the bald-headed gentleman with the long nose was Sir Percy Vince, the world-renowned millionaire chairman of United Motors, and to recognize without being told the face of one of the most austere-mannered of High-Court judges.

After a few minutes, Vincent Hamilton strolled back to the cloak-room, with Mr. Jellipot at his side. It was approached by a passage which bent just before the room was reached. An attendant, standing by the bend, could observe anyone approach while they were yet ten yards away. Those who entered from the street must come up stairs which another attendant could overlook.

The man behind the cloak-room counter looked at the stranger at Mr. Hamilton's side. Mr. Hamilton gave a slight nod.

The man said nothing, but lifted a flap in the counter, through which they passed. He put a key into a door beside the hat-rails, which looked as though it might give entrance to a large cupboard, or an ante-room for the staff. They passed through it to a lighted passage, and it closed quickly and quietly behind them. It would have been impossible for their entrance to have been observed or suspected by anyone but the attendants concerned.

Mr. Hamilton led the way to a brilliantly-lighted room in which two gambling-tables were surrounded by seated players, and outer rings of others who stood and watched. There were excited exclamations at times, but the general atmosphere was quiet and orderly, players and spectators alike having their attention concentrated upon the rolling ball at one table, and the spinning wheel at the other.

There was a refreshment buffet at one side of the room. At the farther end were two doors, one of which led to a room in which baccarat was played. The other was that of the manager's office.

Hamilton said: "If you'll look round for a moment? I shall be back in two minutes. I must let them know you are here." He went into the manager's room.

The manager, Mr. Gordon Ponsonby (a name to which he had a right of an exceptional kind, it being his by his own selection rather than from some remote ancestral chance of residence or occupation), was a large, square man with a hard professionally good-humoured face, and a geniality that could be changed in a moment to a merciless freezing stare. He was too wise to carry arms in the London streets, but here, in his business hours, his right hand would seldom be far from the place where his pocket bulged. He represented Sir Edward Linch, the tube manufacturer, who had received a baronetcy two years earlier, in recognition of his munificent donations to London charities, and who (as was not generally known) had recently acquired a controlling interest in the Cactus Club.

"Evening, Gordon," Vincent Hamilton said, with more familiarity than most men would show when they met Mr. Ponsonby in his own lair.

"Evening yourself," Ponsonby answered, but with a curtness of tone which discouraged any suggestion of intimacy.

"Better get busy outside. There's some pretty high playing going on tonight, and one or two fresh faces here. But you should have been here before this."

"I've brought you a new customer. I suppose he's worth the usual commission?"

"Who's he?"

"Mr. Jellipot. He's a well-known lawyer. Bachelor. Middle-aged. Never seen a gaming-table before."

"And be ringing up Scotland Yard tomorrow?"

"No. He's not that sort. He's in a funk lest it comes out that he's been to a place like this, and his name on the front page of the *Evening Standard* next afternoon. Besides, I've told him to play carefully the first night, till he finds a system that works, and to watch what I do, and follow the same lines."

"You don't mean us to get much profit from that?"

"Not tonight. But I'll see that he plays low."

"He'll come back?"

"How many don't? Especially when they've won a bit, but not much."

Mr. Ponsonby turned to where a thin and nervous young man sat at a desk in the farthest corner of the office, which could not easily be approached without passing the solid obstacles of Mr. Ponsonby's own desk and chair and their formidable occupant. He said: "Give him ten. Number 7. Commission J."

The laconic instructions had no ambiguity to the man who received them. He understood that he was to hand Mr. Hamilton £10, and that he had been told the cryptic manner in which the payment was to be entered in the cash-book before him. He pulled open the door of a safe that was let into the wall at his left hand. He took out a cash-box, from which he abstracted ten £1 notes, and passed them over to Vincent Hamilton in a long thin-fingered hand that trembled slightly. He entered the transaction with an astonishing neatness. It seemed that his fingers regained steadiness when he grasped a pen.... He had been the chief ledger clerk in the bill department at the head office of the London & Northern bank six years before. After that, he had had something over four years in a convict prison. Then a year of dissipation on the money that had been safely hidden till he should come out. Then a bout of gambling in which the remainder had disappeared as quickly as it had been obtained by the forgeries of six years before—and so now he was here.

Vincent Hamilton took the money in a dissatisfied silence. He had expected more. The service of bringing men of the right kind through those fatal doors was one for which Ponsonby would usually pay with greater liberality. The manager saw his expression, and added: "If he cuts up well, you can come again. You know that, Hamilton." His teeth showed as he spoke in a smile in which his eyes had no part.

Vincent said: "Thanks. I'll be reminding you of that before long," and went back to find Mr. Jellipot. It was not his primary intention to enrich the gaming tables from Mr. Jellipot's pockets. It might, indeed, be against his interests to allow such a thing to occur, and the confidential information he had already given to his solicitor as to the methods by which the wheel was spun might be considered an invincible obstacle to such a sequel.

But he was not likely to tell Mr. Ponsonby of that betrayal. And it was well to be in such a position that there would be profit to him from whatever development might occur. He knew, from an experienced observation, that even certain knowledge that a gaming-table is not honestly run will not keep men away when the spirit of gambling has stirred their blood. They will persuade themselves that fortune or their own wits will still be sufficient to bring them home....

He found Mr. Jellipot at the roulette table. He was standing behind one of the players, absorbed in the drama of chance or fraud which he made as yet no effort to join.

An obsequious attendant had already drawn his attention to the greater comfort which was offered by some vacant chairs at the lower end of the table, but Mr. Jellipot had replied, in his diffident manner, but with no lack of finality in his words, that he was waiting for a friend, and preferred to remain standing till he should arrive.

"There can be no system," Mr. Jellipot began at once, showing that his mind had been busy in that short interval, as Vincent Hamilton came to his side—"there can be none which will permanently triumph over a margin of two percent. That must be mathematical fact, and to doubt it would be to doubt the foundations of reason itself. But it would be too dogmatic to assert that no system can be devised which would be of some temporary utility, and by which fortune might be won if it were judiciously used, and were not continued beyond the natural limits that it allows.

"There is, for instance, the method of the doubled stakes. It is evident that, if a man continue to bet on the same colour, doubling his stake on each occasion, he must win, sooner or later, the sum of his first hazard. That is only to say that red or black will not turn up continually, although it may be mathematical fact that the chance of either turning up is not influenced by that which occurred previously, and that there is therefore no certainty that the same colour may not be repeated for a million consecutive times."

Vincent Hamilton, a man of wits which were normally alert in a fallow mind, was quick to conclude that these reflections were the fruit of longer cogitation than the short period of his absence in the manager's room. He saw that Mr. Jellipot must have given considerable thought, not only to the ethics of gambling, but to its practical issues, since they had arranged to come out together; and he knew that the solicitor might be in a peril of which he would not easily be convinced. For when a man begins to theorize about systems, he is halfway to the folly of demonstration, by which he may lose more swiftly than will those who woo fickle chance in a random way.

"I've seen," he said, "long runs of red or black before now, and when you come to doubling the stakes—well, you'd soon be putting up fifty thousand to get back a pound. And a hundred thousand next time to recover that.

"But I don't say you wouldn't get back the pound if you went on. I suppose that's the reason they have a limit above which you're not permitted to go."

"I have no doubt," Mr. Jellipot replied, "they protect themselves, as, apart from fraud, they are entitled to do."

As they spoke, Mr. Hamilton had led the way to a place where there were two vacant chairs, which a watchful attendant was quick to draw out for their accommodation.

Vincent did not slip quietly into his place, as one might do who would not disturb the game. He called a greeting to a man three seats away. The croupier looked up at the sound of his voice, and spoke also. Without exaggeration of emphasis, the players were made aware of his presence. The game paused a moment while he and Mr. Jellipot were supplied with counters, of which Vincent purchased to a value of £10, and Mr. Jellipot, as one who followed a more experienced guidance, did the same. When they commenced to play, three or four of those who were standing around had drifted to the backs of their chairs.

At this table, the single stakes were not usually high, but the pace was fast. A roulette wheel is soon spun. The banker was brisk. He was a man of cheerful manner and lively speech, very quick at joke or retort. He would have made a good auctioneer. He created an atmosphere in which (especially after a few visits to the buffet) it did not seem very important whether you lost or won. Those to whom money came easily might wake up next morning in the same mood. They had had their fun. If they came once a week, and lost three times out of four (in which event they were unusually fortunate men) they might not be clearly aware that they lost on balance at all. And, anyway, it was the luck of the game. It was their own fault, if they plunged at times. Careful players would come out on the right side. There was Vincent Hamilton, for instance, who made no secret of the fact that he kept himself very comfortably on the profit the tables gave. It might have been a prudent (though perhaps hardly a sporting) thing to do to follow his lead. But the fact was that he would stop playing if there were too much of that. He said that it made him nervous and spoilt his luck; and it was a fact that his successes would cease if others began to wager on the same numbers as he.

The roulette wheel, though visible to all the players, was at the upper end of the table. Before Mr. Jellipot spread an elaboration of small white-bordered squares on which he might stake as he would, with a wide range of risks, from that of odd or even numbers, which was approximately an equal chance of winning the stake he played, to the backing of one number alone, with a remote chance of winning a much larger sum. Or he could play, if he would, so that he would win if the winning number were any among ten, which was a popular hazard to choose. He was surprised at the speed and the practised skill with which the game was made, the wheel spun, the winnings calculated and paid, and the lost stakes swept away.

Everything seemed to be accurate, competent, fair. There were no disputes or hesitations. Neither was there the atmosphere of tensity and strain which he had expected to see. The prevailing spirit was that of a rather exciting, rather absorbing, rather jovial game. It was clearly not the etiquette of the room to show emotion for the loss of the stakes that were swept away. They were mere counters of little worth.

The counters were of a separate value of five shillings. He saw Vincent put eight of them on a level chance, and added four of his own. The wheel spun, the counters were raked away and Vincent repeated the stake. Mr. Jellipot thought he would try what independence would do. He staked on 37, and lost. He saw Vincent receive his gains. Vincent put four counters on a ten-to-one risk, and he did the same. A moment later forty counters had been added to his diminished pile.

Mr. Jellipot played for an hour. Frequently, though not always, he duplicated his companion's stakes. Frequently, though not invariably, he won. He was not too absorbed in his own game for eyes and mind to be alert to the significances of the unfamiliar scene.

He considered the implications of the information that Vincent Hamilton had given him, and decided that, if the wheel were dishonestly manipulated, it was very skilfully done. Probably it was no more than an occasional interference, to avert the danger of heavy loss, or to give a winning number to Vincent Hamilton, or any other who might be there in the interest of the management to support the game. Obviously, men would not play if they never won. Obviously also, an occasional pressure upon the scales of chance, made at the most critical times, would add enormously to the percentage of gain which the bank would levy upon the quickly-repeated stakes.

He played for an hour, and had no occasion to buy further counters. At the end of that time his little pile was more than doubled. There had been fluctuations of loss and gain, but the balance had been favourable to him. Vincent had won rather less. Most of Mr. Jellipot's excursions in independence had been disastrous, but these losses had been more than offset by one fortunate coup, when he had staked two counters on a single number, and by luck or the croupier's will it had won.

Vincent, who had eyes for others than those who sat round the table, asked: "Had enough of this?" He looked at Mr. Jellipot's pile of counters, and then at his own, and the solicitor understood him to imply that they had done well enough. He remembered the promise of limited winnings on which he had come, and rose readily.

"We'd better cash in first," Vincent said, "and then have a look at the other rooms." Mr. Jellipot received back the sum which he had invested in counters, with an addition of £11 15s. which he accepted with some satisfaction, chastened by a doubt as to how he should enter it on the orderly and well-balanced pages of his private accounts, and then cheered by the following realization that it would not be liable to income tax, and was therefore equal to fifteen guineas of professional fees.

"I expect," Vincent said, "you'll like to see the baccarat room. There's higher play there. I've seen thousands change hands in a night, though it's a matter of hundreds mostly, unless Lord Henry's there, or one of the other plungers. Sir James Haslet comes here sometimes."

"You don't mean the famous surgeon?"

"Yes, that's he. Next to the barristers, the big medical men are about the best patrons of these places. Money means nothing to them. And they're among the few who can keep it up. Whatever they lose, they know there'll be plenty more to be picked up on the next day. I dare say you'll see one or two lawyers you know."

They had entered the room by this time, and Mr. Jellipot saw that he had been told no more than the truth.

As he looked at the faces of those who sat round the table, he was conscious of a feeling of surprise, of incongruity, which his reason did not support.

He saw Clifton-Waring, K.C., whose fees in the recent Kruman case were said, in legal circles, to have exceeded £30,000. Clifton-Waring was winning. He sat with a hard-jawed dominant face somewhat thrust forward over the table, as though by force of will he controlled the cards. As Mr. Jellipot looked at him his expression relaxed, as a little heap of chips was pushed toward him to augment those that were neatly arranged before him already in larger piles.

He pushed back his chair. "I always stop," he told a neighbour, "when I've won £500, or when I've lost that amount. A man's a fool if he tempts fortune too far."

"When you lose?" the other replied, with a laugh in which the note of envy was plain to hear, "I didn't know that you ever did!"

"Oh, yes, I do," the great man replied, as one who can afford to acknowledge ironic fact. He made his way easily through a crowd of shorter men than himself. Mr. Jellipot's glance left him to observe two other players who sat on the farther side of the table. He thought he recognized in one the features of the great surgeon, Sir James Haslet, who had been mentioned a few moments before, and which were frequently illustrated in the daily Press. He was more sure of the other, Sir Lionel Tipshift, whom he had seen in the witness box at the inquest of Friday last.

They conversed at times as men on a footing of familiar intimacy, which was likely enough between those who were eminent in kindred activities of the same profession. They played variously, being alike only in the fact that they were losing, Sir James moderately, Sir Lionel in larger sums.

Mr. Jellipot saw them both call for further chips, for which Sir James paid with bank notes from a wallet which was still far from empty, and Sir Lionel scribbled an I.O.U.

After that, Sir James began to play recklessly, and his chips were soon done. He rose with an irritation he was at no care to conceal. "Damn it!" he said to Sir Lionel, in a voice which could be heard by many others around. "I wouldn't mind if I ever won!"

Sir Lionel answered without heat, as one who looked from a height upon mundane things: "Well, James, it is the luck of the cards. There would be no game if we were always to win. And we all know it's nothing to you."

His words and manner were without tone of offence, but in that very aloofness there was rebuke. He went on playing in his previous impassive manner, giving another I.O.U. for a further supply of chips. He had one brief run of success, on the coming of which he began to plunge with heavier stakes, so that, as it lapsed, his gains were soon swept away.

Mr. Jellipot, who had continued to watch Sir Lionel's game with an interest which Vincent did nothing to interrupt, now saw him rise with the same serene dignity with which he would enter the witness-box to give his impartial testimony for the prosecution. He went calmly to the door without pausing at the cashier's desk to redeem the I.O.U.'s which he had signed during the evening, and the cashier, observing his withdrawal, pinned them together, and sent them into the manager's office.

He passed Vincent Hamilton on his way out with a closeness which Mr. Jellipot, observing his companion's movements, decided to have been deliberately intended by the latter gentleman, who greeted the scientist with a familiarity which (Mr. Jellipot thought) was not gladly received, although there could be nothing to resent in the cold courtesy of his reply.

When he had gone, Vincent counted £10 from his own winnings, which he handed to the solicitor. "That'll be what you want for Nick Wall," he said. "I'll drop in during the afternoon, or the next morning, to pick up the receipt."

"I cannot, of course," Mr. Jellipot replied, with his usual precision, "give you any assurance that so small an offer will be accepted, but having the first instalment in hand, will give me that confidence which—"

"Oh, they'll take it," his client replied easily. "You'll be more than a match for them. And, besides that, they'd be mugs if they let it go."

"—the position requires," Mr. Jellipot went on, as though the interruption had not occurred. "But I shall be glad to see you, in any event. There are one or two points on which I am still anxious to have your advice."

"You mean about Ada?" Vincent replied, showing no reluctance to develop the conversation in that direction. "I've told you that I'll do anything that I can, if Ada won't think that I'm butting in where I'm not asked. I should say she's in the soup now, and it's getting a bit thick, but you can tell her from me that she'll be none the worse when they've drained it off."

Mr. Jellipot considered this curious use of a common metaphor, and could not be less than pleased by its optimistic conclusion.

"I have some confidence," he rejoined, "that her innocence will be fully established when the entire facts have been ascertained." As her solicitor, it was, perhaps, the least that he could be expected to say.

Vincent answered with more emphatic assertion: "Of course it will. She's not the sort to get up to that kind of trick. Any fool ought to be able to see that."

They went out together, and parted on reaching the street, Mr. Jellipot having a vague feeling that he had gained knowledge of value, and that his investigation had advanced, without being clear as to what the added knowledge or the advance might be. Was it the lateness of the hour, the unusual experience of the gaming-tables, which had excited and confused his mind? He had hoped to make occasion to talk to Vincent tonight, but now he felt that it would be better to defer it to the morrow as he proposed. Let him first have time to clarify his own mind.

CHAPTER XXI.

IT was 4:15 A.M. when Mr. Jellipot buttoned his pyjamas and got into bed, with a resolution that he would sleep at once, so that he should be fit for the work of the next day, as his reputation, and his duty to his clients required.

But he found that routine is more easy to break than to resume. The unsolved enigma of Mrs. Hamilton's murder was a problem which would not retire from the untimely activity of a brain that refused rest.

"Or, at least," as he corrected himself, in a way that showed that he had not abandoned precision of thought in this activity of over-excited nerves, "not of Mrs. Hamilton's murder, but the anonymous letter relating thereto. For if that be traced, it is not easy to think that much mystery would remain, nor could any investigation of the murder be considered complete, nor any verdict, either of acquittal or condemnation be considered satisfactory, while the mystery of its authorship remain unprobed."

And he knew that he himself, and he believed Inspector Combridge also, were as far as ever even from an intelligent guess of who that author might be.

Inspector Combridge would have liked to cast Vincent Hamilton for the part, in view of the impossibility of saddling him with the murder itself, but he admitted that he had no evidence of fact, no theory of probability, to support the wish. And it would approach fantasy to continue the pursuit of such a theory now that Vincent was found to be voluble and emphatic in his cousin's defence.

There seemed more reason in the idea that the letters had been written by someone connected with the firm of Lobbs & Rider. Someone who had overheard incriminating conversation between Ada and Philip North, or who had observed the abstraction of the fatal drug. But to recognize this probability was but a short way upon the path of discovery, and it was open to an objection which Ada Hamilton's solicitor must not fail to observe, that the supposition on which it rested was not easily separable from that of his client's guilt. Merely to direct his enquiries in that direction might be regarded as an admission of the strength of the case against her.

Had the result of the autopsy been of an opposite kind, had it appeared that the first letter was the false invention of a malicious mind, then the dentists' staff would have been the natural suspects among whom to look, but now—well, if the truth were in that direction, it must be left for others to lay it bare.

And if he believed in his client's innocence, as he was half inclined, and must encourage himself to do, then the solution must be of another kind, and the question rose, even if Vincent Hamilton could not be the author himself, did he know, or had he reason to suspect, whom it might be?

Anyway, Vincent was a sufficient problem to intrigue his mind in these wakeful hours, for he was not easy to read.

Mr. Jellipot had thought to use him, and was not sure that he himself was not the one who was being used. He knew what he wanted of Vincent, but he could not see so clearly what Vincent should want of him, and he was always wary of the unknown, as his profession will teach its best disciples to be. Inspector Combridge had said that Vincent Hamilton had outwitted the Yard—or perhaps it would be fairer to say that he had outwitted the law—in an act of audacious fraud, and there was a plain warning there for one who had no overconfident faith in his own powers, in a field where he had little practice, though he could look backward on some success, which might have been no more than beginner's luck.

Why had Vincent invited him tonight to the Cactus Club? There were several possible reasons. He might have had no more than the simple motive of doing him a good turn, by showing him how he could win, though it was to be no more than a moderate sum. But that seemed an inadequate explanation. Holding the position he did, it must at least be an exceptional thing for him to invite another to share his stakes. It was a course which evidently could not be developed far without bringing him into conflict with the management, on whose goodwill his income must entirely depend.

Had he invited him there with the opposite purpose of seeing him become a victim of the gambling lure? Was he perhaps (here Mr. Jellipot came near to one part of the truth) actually paid for bringing him through those guarded doors?

It was true that it would be a singular method of introduction to tell him in advance that the wheel was not fairly spun, but Vincent was not a man who was likely to proceed in orthodox traditional ways. Suppose the whole tale were an invention to give Mr. Jellipot confidence in his first adventure upon the green-baize table of chance? An absurd idea? Well, after all, it had been successful. It had taken him there. He supposed that many men, having gone once, and having money at hand, and none but themselves to consult, would not find it easy to keep away.

He disliked this idea, that he might be dancing to Vincent's tune even while he thought that he could be making use of him, and he saw evidence of his client's cleverness in the fact that he could not even reach a settled opinion as to what the truth might be—that he was only vexed by the suspicion of something he could not probe. And in his search for that which might have no existence outside his over-excited imagination, he dwelt upon the fact that Sir Lionel Tip-shift had been there.

Was there some hidden purpose, some connection in this? He had been surprised at first to see the professional Government wit-ness seated at a night-club gaming-table; but reason told him that prejudice rather than logic had occasioned that first surprise.

From among whom would the amateur gamblers, on which such establishments must depend for their profits, be generally drawn?

First, no doubt, from young men who inherited money without understanding either its value or use: who supposed its great advan-tage to be that it would enable them to lead a life of pleasure rather than toil. But most of them would be quickly fleeced, and when this had been done once it would be for the last time, for it would be cer-tain that they would lack wits to grow a second crop of wool on their own backs.

A different, and more permanently lucrative set of victims would be found among those who made money with such ease that a sense of its real value would be difficult to maintain, and who could lose it with the indifference of knowing that there would be more to be got tomorrow than they would know how, or would have leisure to spend.

Among these, the successful barrister, the popular surgeon, would be prominent, for who beside can earn such fantastic sums in a few hours or a week? They are busy men, having little leisure to spend, and when they do so, it will tend to be at the pace at which the easy money was gathered in.... He had a Harley Street doctor among his own clients who dropped money on the Stock Exchange as ripe plums drop from a tree. When a stock was in demand, and its price was high, he would buy heavily, following the crowd. When he read that it slumped, he would telephone his broker to sell at once. There must be such men, to lose what the wiser gain.... And he saw that the gamblers at the Cactus Club played the same game in another way.

That he had been surprised on first seeing Sir Lionel Tipshift there, was only evidence that he suffered from the common English defect of regarding a man in one aspect alone. Sir Lionel was one whose name was known to a nation of newspaper readers, of whom a much larger proportion would have been unable to state that of the Speaker of the House of Commons or the President of the Board of Trade. He was the expert witness whom the Government would always put into the box to support a prosecution for murder. He had been one among a score of well-known specialists when he had been selected for this curious office, and, because he had been so selected, and had received a title to support the dignity of his appearances, his had become a name to which juries listened with awe. Judges accepted his calm and confident opinions with their maximum gravity, and even defending counsel were deferential in the cross-examinations which their briefs required. It was an atmosphere in which diffidence would not easily flourish, and Sir Lionel Tipshift had never been a diffident man. Every year had increased the air of calm finality with which he had announced opinions heavy with the fate of his fellow-men, and every year had crystallized the public conception of a scientist, able, coldly impartial, indifferent to the results of the evidence which he gave.

But the public conceived him in this aspect only, and Mr. Jellipot saw that, whether it were natural in itself, or a deliberate pose by which his value as a Crown witness was much increased, it left much unrevealed. The public did not conceive him as married or single, generous or mean, a city dweller or a lover of country life. It would have been an incongruity had he published a volume of devotional poems, or entered his name as a competitor in a dirt-track race.

To the public, his private life, his financial or domestic circumstances, simply did not exist, but Mr. Jellipot saw that there must be a background to such façades; and that there was nothing astonishing, nothing even improbable, in the fact that the man who was a brilliant analyst during the day should gamble during the night.

But this reasonable perception did not explain why Vincent Hamilton (if Mr. Jellipot's suspicion were right) should have wished to draw his attention to Sir Lionel's weakness. Even assuming Vincent were honest and energetic in his professed desire to assist his cousin (which Mr. Jellipot was disposed to think), of what use could such knowledge be?

Did Vincent suppose, in the very probable event of Ada being prosecuted for her stepmother's murder, that he could discredit a vital witness for the Crown by charging him publicly with gambling in illicit haunts of the night? The idea was absurd, and could only spring from ignorance of the laws of evidence and the legitimate limits to which cross-examination may go.

Yet to Vincent it might have appeared in a different light; and with the moderate satisfaction of mind that this possibility gave, Mr. Jellipot passed into a belated and needed sleep.

CHAPTER XXII.

THE events of the remainder of the week which must be chronicled were numerous, and of a cumulative importance, though none was of an immediately decisive character. They may be compared to the movements of hostile forces on the day before battle joins. Unobtrusive dispositions are made which may ultimately secure victory or entail defeat. They are observed from the other side, and the opposing forces are advanced, extended, or drawn away. The battle may be decided while the onlooker asks impatiently, "When will the trumpets sound?"

Among events which cannot be recounted in a strict chronological order, precedence may be given to the contribution of the Assistant-Commissioner, who had an idea.

He sent for Inspector Combridge, and was gracious enough to approve his report, and to praise both the ability which had done much, and the discretion which had done no more.

He neither disclosed the contents of the second anonymous letter, nor attached overmuch importance to discovering the author of these communications. He considered that, however momentous the consequences of the first might have been, it had done its part in calling attention to the crime. He observed, soundly enough, that such documents could not be put in evidence (if at all) without the consent of the defence, which, in such a case as this, could not be anticipated.

It had proved to be impossible to trace the writer. Probably that position would continue. Let them face the problem as though those letters did not exist. How did it stand? Mrs. Hamilton had been murdered, and that the poison had been administered by her stepdaughter was beyond reasonable doubt. Was it capable of legal proof? Almost, if not quite. It was a case where a jury's verdict would be hard to forecast. A little more—a very little more evidence would be sufficient to make the criminal's condemnation sure.

There remained the more difficult question of Philip North's probable complicity. As the case stood against him, it amounted to suspicion only, and prosecution might be too dangerous to attempt. If, under such circumstances, he could be induced to confess that he had been a party to procuring the drug, acting in innocence of the purpose for which it would be used, and were allowed to give evidence for the Crown—? Might it not be better to make certain of the conviction of one criminal than to risk that both might slip through the meshes of the net? The inspector did not think that Philip North would be likely to play the allotted part? Well, perhaps they might find other means of building up the case to the strength required. Here the Assistant-Commissioner produced his idea.

"I suppose," he said, "the dosage in the dentistry uses of the drug by local injection is very small?"

"Yes. I have made some enquiries about that. I understand that it is."

"And the amount which was discovered by Drs. Richie and Southfield in the organs of the deceased was very considerable?"

"Yes."

"Then it appears to me that with a drug of this nature—a dangerous and, incidentally, a very expensive drug—it is at least probable that Messrs. Lobbs & Rider will have kept a record of the quantities that the anæsthetist will have used, and that that which should still be in stock will be exactly known. Even in the absence of such records as should have been kept, it may be possible to abstract from the books of the firm the number of times that the drug has been used in the surgeries, and to obtain a sufficiently approximate figure of the stock which should be on hand.

"I conclude," he added, in mild and tolerant rebuke, "from the absence of any allusion to this aspect of the matter in your report that no such enquiry has yet been made?"

"No, I can't say that it has."

"Well, it's an old proverb that two heads are better than one. You'd better get on to it at once."

"And if there should be the expected deficiency in the stock?"

"Which there will: there's no doubt of that. The only question is how carefully they've been keeping their books, and whether they've left any hole to be wriggled through."

"If the evidence appear conclusive on that point, am I to understand that I can then apply for a warrant for Ada Hamilton's arrest?"

"Yes. You can do that. I think that ought to be about sufficient to tip the scale, even if we don't pick up some more as we go on, which you know we most often do."

"But not for Philip North, I suppose?"

"Not without more evidence than we've got now. I only wish that we could."

"Thank you, sir. I'll get on with it at once."

Inspector Combridge retired with a gravely respectful expression, which changed to a slight smile as he reached the outside of the door.

The Assistant-Commissioner's idea was sound, but it was not likely that he would have overlooked so obvious a line of enquiry. But it was his habit to proceed in an orderly manner, and with a sense of responsibility, somewhat different from that of an Assistant-Commissioner who was answerable only to public opinion and the Home Office.

To ask Lobbs & Rider to check their books in such a way, unless it should be a general request to the dentists who had purchased the drug, would amount to an almost direct accusation of murder against Ada Hamilton, and could not be made without that explanation being given, or at least implied.

It was a course not to be lightly or prematurely taken, and when Mr. Jellipot had proposed enquiry as to the total sales of the drug in the London area, the inspector had seen it to be a step which would either render a call upon Lobbs & Rider unnecessary, by disclosing another channel through which the drug had been bought, or supply him with the data for the general enquiry in which they would be included, and would receive the early and particular attention which the circumstances requires.

He was, in fact, only waiting for Sir Henry's reaction to his report, before making the call upon Messrs. Lobbs & Rider which was now suggested, but he was too prudent to assert this intention. He knew that the Assistant-Commissioner would be in better humour if he were left to the belief that he had thought of something which had escaped the attention of the officer in charge of the case; and as the result of this enquiry was to determine the question of Ada Hamilton's arrest, it removed the weight of responsibility from his own shoulders to that of his superior to a very gratifying degree.

He therefore telephoned immediately, and receiving a reply that Mr. Lobbs was in and could see him in half an hour, he took a car to Corbin Street, and was soon being introduced to that gentleman, who received him with a nervous irritability which warned him that he must avoid any provocation of ill-chosen words, or he might fail to obtain any genuine co-operation for the enquiry on which he came.

"I expect," he began, in his most conciliatory manner, "that you have anticipated the matter which brings me here, and which, I need scarcely say—"

He was interrupted by an impatient exclamation. "Now why the devil," Mr. Lobbs exploded, with a lifting of heavy eyebrows, "should you expect that?"

Inspector Combridge saw that he had made a bad start. He began again: "The circumstances of the Hamilton case, with which I am sure you must be familiar—"

The name appeared to rouse Mr. Lobbs to quickened interest, and a second interruption.

"Hamilton case? I don't know what you mean. Nothing wrong with Miss Hamilton, I suppose? One of the nicest girls I ever met. She's coming back on Monday, and very glad I shall be, after the time we've had while she's been away."

Inspector Combridge was puzzled by an attitude which was difficult to accept literally. He thought it barely possible that Mr. Lobbs had no idea of the subject, if not the particular purpose, on which he came. It appeared more probable that he was assuming that attitude in assertion of the innocence of a girl he liked. Well, he must be humoured, if so; but no less must he be required to supply the required information, and it might be worse for Miss Hamilton (and perhaps others of the firm) if it were not done in a willing way.

He began again: "I think, if you will forgive me saying so, that you must have seen from the Press reports, if you have heard from no other source—"

"Press reports? I wish you'd talk in a plain way! I never read Press reports. I've got better things to do. If you'd only—" An idea seemed to enter his mind, at which he checked himself as readily as he had interrupted the inspector before. "I suppose you're trying to tell me that Miss Hamilton's got into some silly trouble with you, and she's sent you here for someone to bail her out. Why didn't you say so at once? It's no use wasting my time. It's Mr. North that you ought to see. He'd bail her out if she'd killed one of your own force, and I suppose you think that's about ten degrees worse than if she'd murdered a child, though why you think you're all so precious valuable is more than I understand."

The words were said without seriousness, and increased the puzzled doubt in the inspector's mind as to how far Mr. Lobbs could possibly be ignorant of the suspicion under which Ada Hamilton lay. But obviously, if so, he believed her innocent, as was evidenced not only by the manner of what he said, but by the fact that he was having her back; not that the inspector was surprised at that, as he had already concluded it to be the subject of the dispute between her and Philip North which had been overheard.

His theory was that she had felt unequal to going back among those who would look upon her as a probable, even though not a convicted murderess, and that her hardier companion had urged upon her that such an attitude was less consistent with innocence than a guilty conscience, and that, if she wished to turn suspicion aside, she must face her position in a more resolute mood.

Evidently, his arguments had prevailed. It exhibited him as the stronger character, as the inspector had always thought him to be, and subtly supported the theory that he had instigated and planned the crime....

"I'm afraid," he said, "it is a different, and possibly a more serious matter than you suppose. But I am sorry that I assumed that you already knew something about it. If you will bear with me for a few moments, I will explain what the present position is."

Mr. Lobbs said: "Well, I'm listening," with some impatience, as the inspector paused a moment to choose his words, and the point at which his narrative must commence; but after he began he had no further interruption of which to complain. Mr. Lobbs listened with a quiet and grave intentness, and said nothing until Inspector Combridge had explained not only the circumstances of Mrs. Hamilton's death, but the immediate purpose for which he came.

Then he said: "Inspector Combridge, I want you to understand first that I wasn't trying to put you off. This is news to me, and I can tell you that it is rather a shock, though it would take a lot more than you have said to convince me that Ada Hamilton would poison anyone. I shouldn't believe it if you said she'd poisoned a cat, unless you'd got two or three witnesses of good character who had seen it done.

"I don't read the papers—not that kind of thing anyway—and if there's been any talk in the office, it hasn't been when I've been about. But as to checking the stock, there's no difficulty, and I shall be thankful to have it done.

"Let me tell you first that all the drugs are in Dr. Addison's charge. He has his own key, and I can say from my own observation that he keeps the cabinet locked. I've seen him go to it a good many times, and I don't remember him ever doing so without it being necessary to turn the key, nor can I remember seeing the key left in the lock.

"Of course, that's no more than any anæsthetist should be relied on to do, but it's fair to say that I have never observed any negligence, and particularly so because Dr. Addison has been giving me some trouble in other ways.

"There are some duplicate private keys kept in a drawer in the safe, including one to the cabinet in question, and Miss Hamilton had one of the safe keys while she was here. In theory, therefore, she could have gone to the drug cabinet, and it's necessary to tell you that. But that's a long way, as I'm sure you'll agree, from saying she ever did.

"As to checking the stock, I can't say that it's often done, and if it were I should probably ask Dr. Addison to go over it, and take his figures, but there's no difficulty in doing it. I know there's a record of every patient who has been treated with this drug, and it's been very carefully kept, because the thing's experimental; and the dosage has been very exact, in accordance with the instructions the makers give, and Dr. Addison's own experience. I should say that there would be no difficulty in proving that very much less than a fatal dose were missing, if that were really the case.

"And I'm particularly glad that the records are exact, because I feel sure that they will convince you that your enquiries must be made in other directions. If it were a decent subject on which to bet, I'd wager anything up to fifty pounds that the stock won't be out by more than a tenth of a grain, and probably not a tenth of that."

"Well, I won't say I hope you're wrong," the inspector answered, "though, if it isn't, it'll leave me in a worse fog than I am now."

He saw no occasion to doubt the dentist's good faith, and was impressed, even against his own judgment, by the confident tone in which this assurance was given.

Mr. Lobbs telephoned for the books to be brought to his own desk, and he made the necessary abstracts himself, in conjunction with the inspector, to whom he was careful to explain the system on which they were written up. He ended with a calculation of the quantity of the drug which should be in stock, which he wrote down, and handed to the inspector.

"And now," he said, "we will ask Dr. Addison to show us what he has got."

CHAPTER XXIII.

DR. ADDISON, it appeared, had just come in. He was invited to Mr. Lobbs' room, and the position explained.

He was a type familiar to the inspector, for it is one that drifts too frequently on to the rocks of the criminal law. Intellectual capacity, weakness, dissipation with its resultant ill health, were all written plainly on the face of a now obviously worried man.

He did not, like Mr. Lobbs, profess ignorance of the Hamilton case. He only protested, with a vehemence which seemed to go beyond what was natural to the occasion, and which was less convincing than the assurances that the inspector had previously heard, that it was absurd to suspect Miss Hamilton of any connection with such a crime, and that it would be a mere waste of time to check the stock to prove what ought not to be the subject of even a moment's doubt.

"Well, I hope you're right," Inspector Combridge said curtly, to cut these protestations short. "We shall soon see."

"I'm afraid I can't do it now," Dr. Addison replied. "There's a patient must have been waiting already for the last quarter of an hour. We'd better make an appointment for some time tomorrow."

"The sooner it's done," the inspector answered, "the sooner you'll be able to see to him."

"That," Dr. Addison answered, with the first effort of self-assertion which he had shown, "is for Mr. Lobbs to say."

Mr. Lobbs said: "Wait a minute. I'll see what I can do." He rang down to Mr. Riddlestone's surgery, and learnt that the expected patient had not arrived.

Dr. Addison, having no further excuse, if such it were—though a waiting patient may be considered good reason enough—led the way to his own room, where the drug cabinet stood. Inspector Combridge, who had learnt to be of a universal suspicion, observed that he turned the key with an unsteady hand, and wondered how much that might be due to his normal condition, and how much to the occupation to which he had so reluctantly come. He watched his movements from that moment with a closeness which would have made evasion impossible, had it been attempted.

But there was no sign of such an attempt, nor would it have been a simple matter under any circumstances. It is possible to make away with a small quantity of any substance in many ways, but it is less easy to improvise it when it is not there.

After the most generous allowance for margins of error, the fact remained that there was a missing quantity of a full three grains, and when Inspector Combridge asked Dr. Addison whether that would amount to a fatal dose, he got the one instant and emphatic reply which had come from that quarter. "Oh, yes. More than that. A lot more. It would kill an ox."

Dr. Addison's apparent reaction to this discovery was one of incredulous bewilderment, and futile suggestion that there must be something wrong with the books, or the calculations which had been based upon them.

Mr. Lobbs appeared to be genuinely distressed, but to face the fact in a more reasonable spirit.

"It shows," he said, when he was alone with the inspector in his own office again, "how you can be deceived when you feel most sure. There are some things that young woman might have done that aren't exactly right, if she'd found herself in a tight squeeze, and I should have been sorry to hear them, but quite believed, and had her back just the same, but as to anything like this—"

His expression, and the gesture of his hands suggested that he was faced by an improbability for which he had no adequate word. Inspector Combridge said: "I know how you feel. I had it sometimes myself when I was new to the game. But you get used to it after a time. We seem to be all much the same till we go wrong."

With this philosophic reflection, born of contact with many criminals of various types, he left Mr. Lobbs, and returned to Scotland Yard, debating in his mind whether the hour had come when he should apply for Ada Hamilton's arrest, or whether he should still delay for a further bag.

He was convinced not only that the crime had been perpetrated as he had first supposed, and as common sense had always urged him to think, but that Dr. Addison had some knowledge of, if not actual complicity in it.

Would an invitation to him to come to Scotland Yard on a strictly "voluntary" visit result in one of those interesting statements which so often assist to fill the docks with the acquaintances of the statement-maker and most often with himself for company, though it may sometimes be prudent to place a constable between them?

There was little danger that a few hours, or even days, of further delay would enable the criminals to escape. They were too closely watched. And it was evident, from Ada's decision to return to her employment, that they had agreed to meet the danger with a bold front, as, in fact, it was most prudent to do.

Indeed, had Inspector Combridge thought that either she or Philip North, or even Dr. Addison, would attempt flight, it would probably have decided him to delay any arrests he might otherwise have made to give them time to commit a folly which went so near to an admission of the guilt which was not otherwise easy to prove.

Being in this hesitation, he resolved to telephone Mr. Jellipot, who, he remembered, had hinted at discoveries which he was hoping to make.

He saw that the result of his afternoon's work could not be hidden for many hours. Even if Dr. Addison were not one of a confederacy of crime, and though he might say nothing of what had been discovered, it was certain that Mr. Lobbs would not hide it from Philip North. So he would be first with Mr. Jellipot to tell that which he could not hide if he would, and hope that it might lead the solicitor to be equally frank with him.

He acted on this decision, the wisdom of which is not open to doubt, but he got a poor crop in return from a barren field.

Mr. Jellipot had had a bad afternoon. He had seen Mr. Wall's solicitors during the morning, and after a telephone consultation with their client in an adjoining room, they had yielded to his courteous but definite refusal even to ask his client to increase the offer which he had been authorized by him to make. It must be taken or left. They could sign judgment in due course, and bankruptcy proceedings would follow? Yes, so they could. It was for them to decide how far their client's interests would be served. They would have the first instalment down, if Mr. Wall should be induced to agree? They could have Mr. Jellipot's cheque at once.

Finally, they had given in, as he had anticipated that they would do. He had made good terms for Vincent Hamilton, in an action to which there was no substantial defence, assisted by the fact that his client had little of character to lose or visible assets on which distraint could be made, and he showed him the receipted terms of settlement, when he called in during the afternoon, with some confidence that it would supply an amicable foundation for the confidence which he hoped to gain.

To a point, so it was. Vincent was too shrewd not to know that, had he gone to a solicitor of lower reputation, such a settlement might have been less easily made. He expressed gratitude of his own kind, and was complimentary in expressions which Mr. Jellipot did not like, but was careful not to resent.

He brought up his cousin's trouble himself, but it was to enquire what Mr. Jellipot was doing to establish her innocence, and to protect her from the blundering threats of the law.

Faced by that blunt question, Mr. Jellipot could not say he was doing much, nor was he willing to discuss the position with more than superficial frankness with one of whom he was still in doubt, particularly as to the discretion with which he would use any confidence which he might receive.

"I hoped," he said, "that your knowledge of the people and circumstances concerned would have enabled you to give me some useful pointers, as I am sure you must be anxious to do."

"I've told you I'll help any way I can, if you mean that, and if Ada wants any help from me. I'm not going to push in where I'm not asked."

"As her solicitor, may I ask you now?"

"Yes. You've done that before, and I said I'd see her any time that she speaks the word. I suppose you've told her that before now?"

"Yes, I told her that, and she expressed her appreciation—I might say her gratitude—for the confidence in her which you expressed."

"Did she say when I could call?"

"She didn't actually mention a time, but I feel sure that she would not resent a visit."

Mr. Jellipot spoke with more hesitation than he allowed to appear. He could not overlook the fact that Vincent was the rival of Philip North, whom Ada had preferred, and he could imagine, from what he had seen of the men, that if the three were to meet it might be unpleasant for all concerned.

Vincent may have had a similar thought, or, at least, a wish to see Ada when she would be alone. He said: "Well, why not ring her now, and fix something up?"

It was a suggestion which Mr. Jellipot could not refuse, though he did it with a feeling that Vincent, rather than himself, was controlling the situation, which caused him a vague resentment. He gave instructions for Miss Hamilton to be rung up, and put through to his own office, and a moment later he heard her voice at the other end of the wire, and here he met with an unexpected check.

Miss Hamilton did not refuse to see her cousin. The terms in which she spoke of him were as friendly and appreciative as they had been before, but she would not be definite as to when he could call upon her. She would telephone to him, and let him know. To-night? No, she would be out till late. Some time tomorrow? Tomor-row would be Saturday. Saturday was always an awkward day. Sun-day? Well, perhaps. But she couldn't say now. It might not be till after Monday. But she would ring him up. What was his number Thanks. She had taken it down.

Mr. Jellipot had to put the best construction he could upon this, but Vincent took it with a sulkiness he made no effort to hide. "I suppose it means," he said, "that she's still carrying on with that boor, and doesn't want me round. I should have thought—" And then he checked himself, as though discretion had reined his tongue. He went abruptly, saying that when she rang him up he'd hear what she had to say, but she might come to wish she'd done so before. He left Mr. Jellipot in doubt of whether he really had any help to give, or had merely been trying to turn the position to his own advantage against his rival, and now showed the spleen of a jealous man.

But he thought Ada had acted with a folly hard to condone. Vincent Hamilton might not be a cousin that every girl would be glad to have, but when one is under grave suspicion of murder, and surrounded by such mystery as she was experiencing, friends of any sort should not be rebuffed without better cause than he could sup-pose her to have.

When Inspector Combridge rang him up a few minutes after Vincent had left the office, he had little information to give him, and was in no mood of satisfaction either with himself or the case which he had in hand. He heard of the missing quantity of the fatal drug as of an extra helping upon a plate of trouble already full, and it was with unusual difficulty that he maintained the tone which is a solici-tor's duty under such circumstances until the last ditch has been lost.

He thought: "Ada did not tell me the truth. She could have seen Vincent before Monday, if she would. Vincent, if he knows any-thing, will not speak, in consequence of her own folly. What chance, under such circumstances, can a solicitor have?

"Yet," he told himself, "she may be innocent, as it is my duty to think, and as I am still half inclined to truly believe. And, if so, there must be an explanation of all these sinister facts which I ought to find.

"Unless, therefore, I exhaust the total possibility of explana-tions, however unlikely they may appear, I fail in the duty which Combridge (who is to be most heartily cursed) has thrust upon me."

He went home in this mood, recalling a possible solution which had come to him during the previous night, and which he had put aside as too fantastic for serious thought. Yet even that must be probed before he could tell himself that the last possibility had been exhausted. He sat long after dinner, taking a second cigar, which he could not recall having done previously, but the only result was that he decided to have some enquiries made next morning concerning Dr. Burfoot, to which further reference need not be made, as they only confirmed the opinion that he had heard from Mr. Lamson, that he was an efficient doctor, and a most respectable man.

CHAPTER XXIV.

MR. JELLIPOT was not one of those numerous professional gentlemen whose offices are left on Saturday mornings in the control of a managing, or sometimes even of a junior, clerk. He went into the city by his usual train, and would remain any length of time that his business required; but that time was rarely more than a couple of hours, and would normally be occupied in balancing his accounts, straightening his desk, and revising bills of costs that his ledger clerk would submit in draft, and preparing generally for an orderly commencement of the business of the following week.

He went in on this occasion at his usual hour, and with a purpose of dealing with several matters which had received meagre attention during the last few days, owing to his preoccupation with the Hamilton mystery. For the moment, that case must be put aside in justice to clients whose business was of almost equal importance, although less dramatic in character, and free from the taint of criminality, which he had always preferred to avoid.

But he was scarcely seated at his desk, and the pile of letters before him was still unopened (for he had an old-fashioned preference for being the first to inspect the correspondence that was addressed to himself), when he was told that Mr. North had called, and was anxious to see him. "He says," the boy who brought in his name added, "that he hopes you won't keep him waiting, because it's very urgent—very urgent indeed."

Mr. Jellipot thought: "So Combridge has taken the plunge at last! Well, it had got to come." He turned over the heap of correspondence, and rapidly sorted out a number of letters the subjects of which were sufficiently indicated by postmark or handwriting. "Take these," he said, "to Mr. Phelps, and ask Mr. North in."

A moment later, Philip North entered the room in a condition of angry agitation hardly controlled.

"I'm sorry," he said. "It's a curse that it's Saturday morning, but something's happened that I want you to deal with at once. I don't know much about these things, but I suppose you can get out a writ, even if it is Saturday, if you do it before midday? What I want to know is whether you can get it out in time to serve it this afternoon?"

Mr. Jellipot perceived that he must adjust his mind. It did not appear probable that this exclamatory opening could be the prelude to an announcement of Ada Hamilton's arrest.

He said mildly: "It sounds rather sudden. Against whom would you wish the action to be commenced?"

"It's against that snivelling cad Lobbs. Pretends he's sorry, and then sends Ada this!"

Mr. North pulled out a letter, which he handed to Mr. Jellipot. He was bursting out into further speech, but checked himself with difficulty in response to the gentle firmness of the solicitor's, "If you will kindly give me time, Mr. North."

But the letter did not take long to read. It was brief in wording, and easy to understand.

15 CORBIN STREET, W.1.
May 15, 19—.

MADAM,

Kindly note that it will be unnecessary for you to resume your duties here next tentatively arranged.

Yours truly,

T. L. L. LOBBS.

Miss A. Hamilton

"I suppose," Mr. Jellipot looked up to say, after a pause a few seconds longer than the actual reading required, "that Miss Hamilton received this letter this morning, and telephoned you for your advice, on which you went to her to discuss the matter."

"You bet I did! Tentatively arranged! The lying scoundrel! Why, I heard him tell her how glad he'd be to see her back in her old place!"

"I suppose you are aware of the circumstance which underlies the writing of this letter?"

"I should say I am! There wasn't much else talked about yesterday afternoon. I gave that drivelling Addison the dressing down of

141

his life. I don't believe he'd know if— To think of taking the word of a man like he! Now if Lobbs had had the sense to give him the sack!"

"I don't think it was exactly a matter of taking his word. But I gathered that he did not make an entirely favourable impression upon Inspector Combridge. That may be a point for us. At present, it is not easy to say."

"Of course it's a bull point. The man almost certainly drugs, and he drinks worse every week."

"Yet he has been kept on by your firm for the very responsible work which I understand—"

"He's a clever man at his job. When he's sober, there mayn't be an anæsthetist in London I'd sooner trust. But he's been warned twice this year that he'd have to clear out if he didn't alter his ways."

"Does Miss Hamilton understand how this letter comes to be written? You made that clear?"

"Yes, of course."

"I asked because your consultation with her must have been short. It can scarcely be more than two hours since she could have received it, and called you up.... I don't say that there may not be a good cause of action, but its expediency is a matter for calmer consideration than it has yet had. And I am sure you will understand that Miss Hamilton's own instructions would be essential before litigation could be commenced."

"We didn't need to say much this morning. We went over all that last night. You can ring Ada up and get her instructions to go ahead in less time that we're wasting now."

"Will you tell me why there is such particular cause for haste?"

"I want this letter withdrawn, so that Ada can walk in on Monday morning without a row. And I don't want Lobbs to go without a headache through the weekend."

"You think that Mr. Lobbs will give way at once if he gets a writ?"

"I think he'll squeal like a stuck pig. He's got a holy horror of law. He once lost seventeen pounds bringing an action against a patient who wouldn't pay."

Mr. Jellipot smiled at that. He said: "An action of this character would be likely to cost him more than seventeen pounds." He had been thinking rapidly while the conversation proceeded, and felt that he was now ready to give the advice that the position required. He went on: "I think I understand how you feel, and, apart from that, I am not sure that you are not right. But if I act in this matter it is necessary that we should be quite clear both as to what we are aiming to do, and the possible consequences which it may entail.

"In the first pace, there is an unpleasant fact, which, in Miss Hamilton's interest, it is necessary for us to face. In the eyes of the police, if not in ours, she is under grave suspicion of being the cause of Mrs. Hamilton's death, and this apparent discrepancy in the stock which is under Dr. Addison's control, and to which she had access, makes that position more serious than it was before. Yes, I know all that you want to say. But it would be loss of time saying it to me, and you want us to get on. My point is that Miss Hamilton may be arrested at any time, and may have to face a trial for murder which, however confident we may be in her innocence, will not be easy to meet."

"That's no reason we shouldn't hit back when we get the chance. It's all the more reason we should."

"Did I say anything contrary to that conclusion? But will you kindly listen to me, and endeavour to follow the argument I am putting before you? I say Miss Hamilton is under the imminent danger of having to defend herself from this most serious charge, and all other considerations should be subordinated to that.

"But it does not necessarily follow that it would be wise for her to accept this dismissal—for such it is, though its wording, perhaps more from kindliness than any inferior motive, is not free from obscurity—without protest, even carried to the length which you propose.

"Suppose, for instance, that she had attempted the folly of flight, it would have been a legitimate, even though not a conclusive, argument that she had acted as a guilty person would be likely to do; and so, if she should react to this dismissal in a spirit of indignant refusal to accept the verdict that it implies, it might influence a more favourable judgment."

"Well, isn't that what I said when I came in? If you see that, I can't see why you don't go ahead at once, as she wants you to do."

"Perhaps, Mr. North, if you would not interrupt we might reach the point in a shorter time. There is one contrary consideration, which I am bound to put plainly. But there is also a further argument for the course which you are so urgent that I should take, and, by your leave, I will state it first, as I was intending to do.

"The point is this. The case, as it stands, is one in which the evidence is strong, but it is yet not such that the police can feel as certain of securing a conviction as they would like to be. Or, at least, that was how it stood twenty-four hours ago, and how far this last development may have influenced them to decisive action I cannot say. But the case is one which they have been disposed to handle warily, because it has a feature which they particularly dislike—a material circumstance (that of the anonymous letters) which they cannot explain, and which puts them in the position of taking a case into court which, on their own admission, they have not thoroughly mastered. If the writer of those letters be beyond discovery, may there not be other facts which have baffled them equally, and which may have a vital bearing upon the crime?

"Now, under such circumstances, it occurs to me that it is barely possible—I should not like to put it more strongly—that if the police should be informed that Miss Hamilton were bringing an action against her employers for defamation of character on the clear issue of whether the imputation that she had caused the death of her stepmother could be sustained, then I say that it is just possible that they might hold their hands until that action shall be decided.

"And, if you will accept this as no more than a rash opinion expressed upon a position to which I have had as yet insufficient time to give the consideration which it requires, I am inclined to think that the justification of such a libel would be a more difficult legal process than would be the obtaining of a verdict of guilty to a prosecution in a criminal court.

"But I said that there is one argument which must weigh heavily in the opposite scale. If such an action should be brought unsuccessfully, so that the jury's verdict would imply that Mr. Lobbs had been justified in his evident conclusion that Miss Hamilton was responsible for the theft of the missing drug, then it appears to me that the police would have no option but to institute a prosecution for murder, even though (about which I am less than sure) they may hesitate to do so under the circumstances we already face."

Mr. North had heard this clear, but somewhat redundantly worded exposition with more self restraint than his previous conduct had led Mr. Jellipot to expect, and now that the solicitor paused, either to recruit his breath, or because he had reached the period at which he had aimed, his client exploded with: "Wouldn't any jury see what it meant? And wouldn't it make them infernally slow to play such a dirty game?"

"Yes. I am inclined to think that it would have a decided tendency to result in a verdict against Mr. Lobbs, unless in the course of his defence he should succeed in absolutely convincing the jury of Miss Hamilton's criminality, so that their sympathies would be alienated from her."

"Well, if all that's as you say, I still think we should go ahead. Ada's in a tight place, and she's got to kick to get out. I say fight all along the line, and let them all know that we're not going to take the thing lying down.

"It's ten thirty-five now, and I suppose there's time enough to get a writ out, and bung it in to him before night. I can tell you where you can get him for sure. He plays bowls most Saturday afternoons, and I know he's got a match on today."

"I am afraid," Mr. Jellipot replied doubtfully, "that even if we adopt the policy which we prefer, and obtain Miss Hamilton's authority, which I have little doubt that we should be able to do, we can hardly proceed with the celerity which your quite natural impatience suggests.

"There is an etiquette in these matters which I, at least, cannot ignore. There is what is known as a 'letter before action' which we cannot omit without prejudicing our own position, and perhaps bringing reflections upon myself which I should prefer to avoid.

"Apart from that, an action of this character is somewhat different from that which claims specific performance of a commercial contract, or the recovery of money owing, and it is usual for the learned counsel by whom the pleadings will ultimately be drawn to settle the wording of the endorsement upon the writ."

Mr. North, for all his impatience, had the wit to see that Mr. Jellipot would only proceed by the beaten path, and that the most he could do would be to encourage him to make haste in his own way. He said: "Well if it's a letter it's got to be, we'd better see that he gets it this afternoon. Give it me, and I won't trust it to anyone else. I'll go over and slap it in."

Mr. Jellipot, though he might decline to be stampeded by the impetuosity of the younger man, was not insensible to the value of speedy action in the position in which they stood. He said: "Perhaps we can do better than that. Do you know where Mr. Lobbs could be reached on the telephone at this time of day?"

"He doesn't come in on Saturday. You'd get him on the phone more likely than not at his own place. It's Putney 0404."

Mr. Jellipot had now decided upon his plan of action. He first telephoned Ada Hamilton, from whom he received an agitated but emphatic authority to do what ever he and Philip might think best to refute the imputation which her dismissal in such a manner implied.

He then called in a stenographer to whom he dictated this letter, to be addressed to Mr. Lobbs, at his Putney residence:

DEAR SIR,

I am instructed by my client, Miss Ada Hamilton, to acknowledge your letter of yesterday, and to point out that the arrangement by which she was to resume her duties with your firm on Monday next was not of a tentative character.

Your partner, Mr. Philip North, who has seen me this morning, confirms this, and wishes to disassociate himself from a letter which was written without his knowledge, and contrary to his judgment.

In the absence of an immediate withdrawal, and a suitable apology, I am instructed to commence legal proceedings against you for the recovery of damages adequate to the libel upon my client's character which your letter implies

Yours faithfully,

E. V. JELLIPOT

"Bring it in," Mr. Jellipot said, in conclusion, "as soon as you have it typed," and then to Mr. North, as the stenographer retired: "If I should now telephone Mr. Lobbs, and read that letter to him before consigning it to the post, can you forecast what his reaction would be?"

"He'll haul his flag down with a run."

"In that case it may be best to phone Inspector Combridge first, while the present position is undisturbed."

Two minutes later, he was connected to Scotland Yard, and recognized the inspector's voice.

"Good morning, Combridge," he said, "I've got a bit of information to give you this time in return for what I had from you yesterday. Mr. Lobbs has written to Miss Hamilton telling her not to go back to the office on Monday."

"Well, what did you expect?" The tone of this question implied that the news was of too obvious a character to have been worth the trouble of ringing him up to tell it.

"I suppose you would connect this letter with the result of your visit yesterday?"

"Yes, of course. That's quite obvious. You don't mean that she's done something else that I don't know?"

"Of course not. I don't mean that she's done anything at all. But in view of the construction that you, and doubtless others, would place upon Mr. Lobbs's letter, he seems to have put himself in a very serious position."

"I'm afraid I don't follow that."

"He has issued a libel which he may find it very difficult to justify."

"You don't mean—? I shouldn't say he'd need to lose much sleep over that."

"I suppose that must depend upon questions of temperament and constitution, of which, after your interview yesterday, you would be better able than I to judge."

There was a moment's silence following this remark, and Mr. Jellipot, fearing that he might appear to rise to a bait that had not been thrown, and added mildly: "Well, I thought you might like to know," and would have terminated the conversation, when the inspector broke out with: "Look here, Mr. Jellipot, you're not wanting to make me believe that Mr. Lobbs has anything to fear from that woman?"

"I have already received instructions to issue a writ for libel in the absence of an immediate withdrawal, and an unqualified apology."

"She'll only make herself look a fool. He'll take no notice of that."

"It is a course of action which has my entire approval."

"It sounds silly to me, unless you've got something up your sleeve that you've been keeping from me."

"No, I don't think I can say that. The position is still one of considerable ambiguity, which the action I am instructed to take may do much to clarify."

He heard Inspector Combridge give an inarticulate grunt, and waited in patient silence for a more intelligent reply, which soon followed.

"I suppose you'll be asking us next not to arrest anyone till we see the result of a libel action."

"It would be a matter for your own discretion rather than a request from me."

The inspector grunted again. "But for you," he said, "I believe I should have run her in any day during this week."

Mr. Jellipot replied cheerfully: "It is a restraint for which you may see reason to thank me before it's all over."

The conversation ended here by a mutual impulse. They both felt that there was no more to be said.

CHAPTER XXV.

"NOW," Mr. Jellipot said, "we will endeavour to have a few words with Mr. Lobbs."

It was Mrs. Lobbs who answered the call. She said that Mr. Lobbs was in the garden, and when he was occupied there he did not like to be fetched in. Was it something that she could do?

Mr. Jellipot replied that it was a matter of urgent business on which he was afraid it was essential that he should speak to Mr. Lobbs himself. Would Mrs. Lobbs kindly let him know that Miss Hamilton's solicitor was on the telephone?

"Oh, yes," she said, in an altered, pleasantly excited voice, "that dreadful Hamilton affair!" and Mr. Jellipot observed that the dentist was not one of those discreet men who avoid talking business at home. "Please hold on a moment," she went on, "I'll send someone to fetch him in."

A minute later Mr. Lobbs announced his presence at the other end of the line. "I am," Mr. Jellipot commenced, "Miss Hamilton's solicitor, and I thought—"

He was interrupted by: "I am sorry that, in view of what I learnt yesterday, it is not a matter in which I am prepared to give any assistance."

Mr. Jellipot perceived that Mr. Lobbs's imagination outran the facts. "I am afraid," he said, "that you are as hasty in your assumptions today as you were yesterday. I am not aware that Miss Hamilton is requiring any assistance, and, in any event, I have no instructions to ask for anything from you, beyond a withdrawal of your letter of yesterday, and a sufficient apology."

"But I— Surely she—" The first astonished exclamations died unfinished and the speaker controlled himself to say more calmly: "I can only conclude that you have been misinformed of what the position is, although Miss Hamilton can hardly have failed to make a good guess, even though she may not have heard of the discovery which was made yesterday afternoon. If you will please inform her that a deficiency of stock in the drug cabinet—"

"Miss Hamilton has already been fully informed of the events to which you allude," Mr. Jellipot interrupted, "but it both simplifies and strengthens the position to have your own assurance that the letter that she received from you this morning—"

"If you are already informed of what has transpired, Mr. Jellifield—?"

"Mr. Jellipot, if you please."

"I beg your pardon, Mr. Jellipot. If you are so informed, you must, I am sure, recognize that I have dealt with the position with all possible restraint and consideration. It appeared to me on reflection that I was not concerned with anything beyond the actual theft which had occurred on my premises, especially as the police already have the matter in hand."

"That being your view, Mr. Lobbs, I am afraid that nothing will be gained by further discussion. But perhaps you would be interested to hear a letter which I have addressed to you already, and which will reach you this evening."

As Mr. Lobbs was not quick to reply to this offer, Mr. Jellipot took silence for consent, and proceeded to read it.

Almost immediately after doing this, and without further words on his side, Mr. Jellipot put back the receiver. He looked up to Mr. North to say: "Mr. Lobbs considers it absurd. He also considers it absolutely ridiculous. He rang off without giving me time to discuss the propriety of these adjectives."

"I bet he's feeling uncomfortable, however he tries to bluster it out. He won't forget what I said to him yesterday afternoon."

"Well," Mr. Jellipot agreed, "his voice did sound rather agitated."

It sounded more so when he came on again a moment later. "Do you ask me to believe, Mr. Jellipot, that I have no right to cancel the appointment of one of my staff, even after an act of the gravest dishonesty has occurred, with a terrible inference which fortunately I am not asked to judge? It sounds preposterous to me."

"I certainly suggest that you are not entitled to dismiss anyone without proper notice, or any opportunity of self-defence, unless you have proof of the dishonesty which you impute. If you are prepared with legal proof of such criminality, you have nothing to fear from the action which I am instructed to bring."

"Do I understand that Miss Hamilton seriously denies having any knowledge of the matter?"

"She emphatically denies having taken anything. She considers that your knowledge of her character should have been sufficient to have enabled you to dismiss such a suggestion as being, in your own words, preposterous."

Mr. Lobbs's voice became weak with indecision, though there was no reason to doubt its sincerity, as he said: "No one would be more glad than myself to believe that the suggestion which has been made against Miss Hamilton—not by me, Mr. Jellipot—by the police, not by me—is without foundation.... I did not think that she would wish to return after the discovery which had been made, even if—I mean, if she had been in a position to do so. But if you tell me that I have acted too hastily—"

"Perhaps," Mr. Jellipot interrupted coldly, not thinking it well to accept too easily a mere verbal surrender, "it will be best for you to send a written answer to my letter after you receive it. It will be sufficient now if you authorize me to inform Miss Hamilton that she will be expected to resume her duties at the usual time on Monday morning."

"Yes. She can do that. I should deeply regret—I mean I should be most thankful—if there should prove to be no foundation for the charge that Inspector Combridge has made."

"Miss Hamilton will give you her own assurance that there is none whatever."

He laid down the telephone, sealed the letter, and handed it to Philip North, who said no more than: "I shall catch him before lunch, if I'm quick," and left hastily, with the expression of a man who was still athirst for his partner's blood.

Mr. Jellipot was left to consider whether he should ring the inspector again, which he was disinclined to do. He would have preferred to leave him under the impression that the matter would be fought out in a court of law. But this hesitation not being sufficiently strong to overcome a scruple of conduct which suggested that such silence would be less than fair, he did ring up Scotland Yard again, and finding, with some slight disappointment, that the inspector was still in, he said: "You will be interested to hear that Mr. Lobbs has agreed that Miss Hamilton shall resume her duties."

"So I suppose there'll be no more talk about actions for libel now?"

"It is too soon to say that. I have not yet seen the letter of apology which Mr. Lobbs has been requested to write."

"I believe you think you'll wriggle that woman out in the end. But I don't think you will."

There was a reluctant admiration mingled with the incredulity of the inspector's voice as he said this, to which Mr. Jellipot responded with his accustomed modesty: "It isn't anything that I'm doing. It's because neither of us can make out what really occurred."

"You might speak for yourself. We're beginning to think that there isn't much that we haven't straightened out now."

"You mean you've found out who wrote the letters?"

"No. I wish I did. That's the one point we've still got to clear up."

Mr. Jellipot was on the point of saying: "Don't you think Dr. Addison might be worth a bit more attention?" but was stayed by the thought that to discover that the letters were written by him might be to dig up a final proof of his client's guilt. Besides, why should he have written them? It was difficult to construct any plausible, even any fantastic theory, which would give him motive for that.

Inspector Combridge, from an opposite angle, had directed his thoughts in the same way, and been held up by the same difficulty.

Mr. Jellipot closed the conversation with a friendly and most sincere wish that Inspector Combridge would go home and have a quiet weekend. He had felt no more than a very limited satisfaction in the morning's events. He thought: "I may bluff, and bluff; but it will make no difference at last, unless I can find some explanation of these events by which my client is cleared. The law wins in the end." And what explanation—except the obvious one—could there be?

He put it out of his mind for a time, recognizing the claims of other matters that could not wait. Perhaps inspiration would come during the weekend.

CHAPTER XXVI.

CHIEF-INSPECTOR COMBRIDGE was often occupied on Sunday by official duties, but he did not expect to be so, unless the circumstances were of an urgency that could not wait. He had a wife of whom he was fond. He had a garden of which (on his wife's own testimony) he was fonder still. He had three children, as red-haired as himself, who might have tied, if not won, against both garden and wife.

But this Sunday his family had gone to visit a married sister at Aylesbury, and while the two ladies, fifty miles away, purred openly over each other's children, and congratulated themselves secretly over the superiority of their own, he was able to work quietly in the potting-shed, until Roberta should call him in to his midday dinner, and to give undisturbed consideration to the problem which was still so incompletely resolved.

It was past the noon hour, and he was beginning to feel a pleasant anticipation of the sound of the bell which the girl would ring at the kitchen door to call him in to the meal that his labours earned, when, very faintly, but with a most damnable certainty, his ear caught the sound of the telephone from the open dining-room window.

The next moment Roberta's voice called shrilly as she ran down the garden path: "Please, sir, you're wanted on the phone."

"It's the office, Berta, of course?" he asked with the resignation of experience, as he returned with her to the house.

"Yes, sir. They said as it were that urgent that I must fetch you wherever you was."

He entered the house with a feeling of certainty as to what he would hear. She (or perhaps they?) had decided to utilize the week-end for the sudden bolt which she (or they) recognized as the sole alternative to the prison cell, the shadow of which was darkening with every hour.

Probably the letter that Ada Hamilton had received that morning, however cleverly Jellipot might endeavour to bluff it out, added to the knowledge of the discovery of the deficiency in the stock of the fatal drug, had been the last straw, and the prudence—or audacity—by which she had held her ground had been submerged in a panic fear.

Well, it showed the soundness of the patient methods which he pursued. It was as effective as the American third-degree, and far preferable in other ways. Now she (or they) would be captured in flight or hiding, and would themselves have supplied the final evidence by which no jury would doubt their guilt.

He had been resolving, as he had mixed the loam for his cherished azaleas, that he would interview Dr. Addison, with no clearer purpose than that of a rat that nibbles, now at one place, now at another, at the wood of a store-cupboard, too hard for its teeth to tear; but now he saw that he would be employed in a better way. All the same, why couldn't people arrange their crimes, and their subsequent exoduses in such a manner that a chief-inspector of the C.I.D. could get his fair allowance of Sunday rest?

Roberta heard him go to the telephone. She heard him say impatiently: "Yes, it's me," with a violation of grammar of which they were as unconscious as was Superintendent Davis at the other end of the wire. After that there was a moment of silence, during which she listened intently, for she took a deep though distant interest in the mysteries of her master's calling. She was rewarded on this occasion, by hearing him exclaim (for he had left the dining-room door open as he had entered hurriedly): "*What*? Killed himself? But why should he? No, of course, you couldn't say yet. Not definitely, before there's a post-mortem. It sounds like murder to me.... Well, yes, if he knew something he mightn't be allowed to tell.... If I might suggest, sir, I'd tell Dr. Feltham not to disturb anything, and get Sir Lionel on it at once.... Yes, I quite understand that, sir. But there was the Warlcott case where he blamed us for not letting him inspect the body at once, and you may say that he's in on this one already.... Yes, I take that for granted. It's linked up somehow.... 62A Clissold Street. Yes, I've got that. I'll go straight there at once."

He called to the listening girl: "Berta, have you got my shoes cleaned? Well then, do them at once, while I change."

He was downstairs again in five or six minutes in different clothes, and with no remaining traces of his recent occupation, being used to meeting these sudden calls.

"You won't go without dinner, sir?" the girl asked anxiously.

"There's some stewed eels that'll be ready almost at once, as you might say."

"I'll wait three minutes, if you'll crank up the car for me while I eat."

But, as he had known before he spoke, her devotion was not equal to so hard a test. She had a horror of cranking cars since her brother Herbert's wrist had been broken by a backfire.

He added: "If I'd had any sense I should have been in Aylesbury today," and with no further protest she let him go, and dished up the eels for a meal in a lonely house....

Dr. Addison had passed the last six months of his solitary drug-ridden life in a high narrow room of a house that had once, in a better time, been a home also: a spacious home of love, of dignity, and of quiet peace.

Now it had not been destroyed by the inflexible verdict of time, but had fallen to a worse fate. It had been split and portioned and modernized into a warren of service flatlets where some score from London's million of homeless women and men were sheltered in single rooms, and warmed, and kept alive for the work of the coming day. And to one of the highest and smallest of these, Dr. Addison, whose considerable income had been strained to provide the drugs which he required in ever-increasing quantities, and which were not procurable, even by a medical man, in simple legitimate ways, had migrated six months before.

Now he lay on his back on a divan bed, with one leg trailing awkwardly over the side (but not hanging, for the bed was too low for that) and a policeman guarded the door.

We need not ask why an intellect which his neighbours praised had been unequal to persuading him from the folly of drugs, the effects of which he had watched in others in the course of his professional work: what tragedy of ill health of body or mind he had striven to forget or to overcome, for our business is not with him. Or, at least, it is no further with him than is necessary to discover the secret of why he died, which Inspector Combridge, in his systematic manner, proceeded to do.

The manageress, Mrs. Hawker, a small, sharp-featured woman, with a veneer of professional affability, was his precedent source of information, and her evidence, with other indications, appeared to establish the tragedy as a case either of suicide or the accidental overdose of a narcotic drug.

Dr. Addison, she said, had taken the room about six months before, and she had recognized him almost at once as a drug-addict—a diagnosis for which such women are exceptionally competent, the

great majority of these unhappy people being found among the oc-
cupants of such barrack-like substitutes for natural home-life as they
control.

He had been, from the first, irregular in his hours of coming in
and going out, concerning which no supervision was exercised, nor
restraints imposed; but his breakfast (the one meal which was to be
regularly supplied, and the cost of which was included in his weekly
rent) was always served at eight-thirty, or nine on Sundays.

It was brought up by a waiter, who had a key to the drop latch,
which he would use, after knocking, if he obtained no reply.

Usually, she was told (but the waiter, Spence, would confirm
this), Dr. Addison would be awake and dressed when the breakfast
tray was taken in. Occasionally, he would be asleep, perhaps lying
on the bed partly or wholly dressed, under which circumstance he
had told Spence to lay the tray down, and leave him undisturbed. On
more than one such occasion he had remained in that condition for
many hours, so that the chamber-maid's morning attentions to the
room had been delayed.

This morning there had been the unusual circumstance that the
catch on the inside of the door had been dropped, so that Spence had
been unable to enter, and after some abortive knocking he had laid
the tray down on the mat.

He had returned half an hour later, when the tray had still been
there, and he had again knocked without result. After that, he appeared to think he had done enough (there was no lift in the building, and the stairs were many), and the next scene in the drama was
at eleven, when the chambermaid, Hannah, had appeared to
straighten his room, and had found the breakfast tray still lying outside.

It was an unwritten etiquette of these service-flatlets that, be the
hours of privacy, of occupation, or absence, otherwise what they
might, there should be freedom of access for the customary morning
ministrations. Hannah turned her attention to the two other rooms
that were on the same landing, and then, seeing that the tray was still
outside, and having knocked without reply, and finding that her key
would not open the door, she had whistled down the speaking-tube
to Mrs. Hawker, who, on coming up, had knocked with more vigour
than Hannah had felt free to use, but with no different result.

Mrs. Hawker had then summoned the hall-porter, and had instructed him to do as little damage as possible in forcing the door.

As it gave way, she had seen Dr. Addison sprawled upon his
back on the bed, with the awkwardly projecting leg, and evidently
unroused by the noise which their method of entrance had required.

155

She had advanced with the words: "I think, Hannah, you'd better phone for Dr. Hill to come round. I think he's been taken ill." But even as she spoke she saw that the time when doctors might help was gone. She had added, quickly: "No, don't do that. We shall have to let the police know."

She had looked through the window, far down to the street below, and seen two policemen on the opposite pavement, moving with the measured solemnity which is part of the ritual of the Metropolitan police when they go abroad together.

A sharp order to the porter had sent him downstairs at a pace which had enabled him to interrupt their leisurely progress before they had reached the street corner, and Sergeant Bickett had thereupon separated himself from his companion, followed the porter's lead at a livelier pace, and taken charge of the event with a prompt efficiency which had informed Scotland Yard, within something under four minutes, of the name of the dead man, and the probable manner of his decease.

The incident, apart from that identification, would have been no more than the routine of the day, but Sergeant Bickett had been sufficiently conversant with the ramifications of the Hamilton case to observe its potential connection with the major mystery, and to ensure that his report should reach an officer who would recognize its importance.

In the result, it had been a police-surgeon only who had been hurriedly sent for the barren necessity of certifying that the dead man was beyond human aid, and, except for him, the room had remained undisturbed and unentered until Inspector Combridge was on the spot.

The inspector heard Mrs. Hawker's account. He heard those of the members of the staff who could support it, and he decided that it would be waste of time to question them further. Whatever more could be learnt would be from the contents of the room itself, and from the body of the dead man.

But he had scarcely concluded these essential though unproductive preliminaries, and commenced a systematic examination of Dr. Addison's papers, with some faint but exciting hope that they might contain illuminating references to a possible knowledge of, if not to any active part in the Hamilton murder, when he was interrupted by the sound of a booming, graciously-condescending voice, and a heavy tread that followed Mrs. Hawker up the stairs. Rather against, and much sooner than his anticipations, Sir Lionel Tipshift had appeared on the scene.

"I'm glad you've come, Sir Lionel," he said, as he met him at the door of the room. "It was, in fact, my suggestion that you should be informed, though I scarcely ventured to hope—and on Sunday too—"

"I was glad," Sir Lionel answered, "to have the opportunity of doing so. In view of the events which have just occurred, as I have been informed this morning, it is difficult to avoid the conclusion that there is a direct connection between Mrs. Hamilton's death and the end of this unfortunate man. The whole case is one of considerable—I may say of exceptional—interest; and I must thank you for giving me this opportunity of being first on the ground.... But, of course," he smiled in his most Olympic manner, "we assume nothing, Inspector; we assume nothing at all."

He had laid down and opened a black bag of considerable size and weight as he said this, and looked comprehensively round the room, with a gaze that missed little of what it saw. He said, rather sharply: "I suppose I really am first, Inspector? Or hasn't there been a G.P. messing around already?"

"There's only been our own Dr. Nuttall. He made a sufficient examination to leave no doubt that life was extinct—though I shouldn't say there's much difficulty in seeing that—and arranged for the body to be taken to the mortuary. I expect by this time there's an ambulance on the way. Of course, that will be subject to your directions now."

The great man pondered a moment. He picked up, and smelled, a hypodermic syringe that lay with other articles, including a small open packet of powder and an empty glass, on a small table beside the telephone at the head of the divan bed. He said: "No. No Perhaps I shall not need to be long here. Let it come by all means.... Perhaps, under the circumstances, if you wouldn't mind letting me have the room to myself for a short time? There are one or two tests I shall have to make, and I always like to work undisturbed. I am sure you will understand that.

"Of course, I shall disturb nothing except this." His hand waved downward to the body over which he towered as it sprawled on the low bed. "I do not intrude upon the deeper mysteries of the craft." He repeated: "The deeper mysteries of the craft," as though pleased with the gracious compliment to the inspector's occupation which it implied, and yet as one who could afford to deprecate the importance of his own work, it being too evident to require defence.

Inspector Combridge said: "Certainly, Sir Lionel I'll let Mrs. Hawker know that you don't want to be disturbed. I'm afraid you can't fasten the door, but I'll tell the constable not to let anyone in. I'll let you know if the ambulance comes."

Sir Lionel's eyes rested on the telephone. "I've no doubt," he said, "that this is an extension from the main service. You can ring me up if it comes."

He threw off his coat, and turned up his cuffs, as he bent over the inanimate object upon the bed, and Inspector Combridge went out, closing a door which would still latch, though its lock was gone, and instructing the stolid constable on the landing to let no one enter without instructions from him.

CHAPTER XXVII.

IT was Monday afternoon when Inspector Combridge sat in Superintendent Davis's room, with the burden of some fresh facts on his mind, but no assurance of the direction in which they led.

"There doesn't seem to be any doubt," he said, "as to how Addison died; nor much about when he made up his mind that he'd got to do it.

"It couldn't have been a case of overdosing himself by mistake, as we know that these drug-addicts are always likely to do, because he didn't die from anything of the kind.

"He died from an injection of the same drug that killed Mrs. Hamilton, and he must have taken a quantity of it from the Corbin Street stock, almost immediately after the discovery that some of it was missing, because he left the premises about ten minutes afterwards and didn't return."

"There's no doubt he had it from there?"

"No. No reasonable doubt. There's a further quantity missing. More, Sir Lionel says, than would be required for a fatal dose."

"Were they expecting him to return?"

"No. There was nothing out of order in that. He had no engagements there for Friday after the patient who didn't keep his appointment, and he's never there on Saturday mornings."

"You say he took the drug on Friday, and didn't kill himself until a late hour on Saturday night. Doesn't that suggest that, even if he thought of doing so when he took it, it was less than a settled resolution at that time? Have you traced what he did during Saturday? Do you know whether he got in touch with Ada Hamilton, or anyone else who may have been connected with the Hamilton murder?"

"Not so far as I can ascertain, but of course that would be difficult to prove. There's always the possibility of the telephone, and if a man's not being shadowed—but I needn't explain that to you."

"But he should have been shadowed, after what had been found out, and his reluctance to have the stock checked."

"Yes. I see that now. You can't kick me harder than I'm kicking myself. But there wasn't any definite display of reluctance beyond the fact that he said he had a patient waiting, which he no doubt believed to be true.

"And there really wasn't any reason to think that he came into the case to an extent which could cause him to take his life, even if he were in it at all, which didn't seem probable. There was no motive that I could see, especially as Ada Hamilton could have got the drug without asking his leave, and at much less risk to herself than by taking him into her confidence. You can find a motive for North, but not him.

"And as to his getting in touch with her, you must remember that we've got men watching both her and Philip North wherever they go."

"Yes. I don't overlook that. But perhaps you'd better go on telling me what you have discovered, instead of my asking you what you haven't."

"I've found out that he went to the Grim Street branch of the London & Northern Bank on Saturday morning, and closed his account. He drew out a balance of twenty-two pounds four and six."

"That looks more like bolting than suicide."

"He went on to the post-office at the corner of Grim Street, and bought a money order for twenty-two pounds in favour of a sister, Rachel Addison, who lives in Belfast. As I haven't been able to find it, we may presume that he posted it to her. Apart from that, he appears to have been possessed of about twenty-five shillings when he died."

"Well, that looks more like a plan to commit suicide than to bolt."

"Yes. I think it's conclusive. Apart from that, I can't say that he left any documentary evidence. I spent half the night going over his papers. There were no farewell letters, or anything of that kind. There's no will, unless it's deposited elsewhere, but that's not surprising, if he'd got nothing to leave."

"Then you found nothing to connect him in any way with the Hamilton case?"

"Nothing whatever. There was a good deal of correspondence that I had to go through, but the bulk of it was years old. And there were a lot of technical notes on his own job, and what looked like the manuscript of an unfinished book that he'd tried to write at a time when his hand was firmer than it had become since, and there were odd memoranda of no importance from our point of view, such

160

as addresses of dentists, from whom he probably tried to get employment as an anæsthetist similar to that he had in Corbin Street."

"Nothing about the anonymous letters?"

"Not an indication of any kind. I think I can say that I've established that as soon as the deficiency of the stock was discovered, he decided that self-destruction was the only way out of whatever mess he was in, but I can't go beyond that yet."

"Any theory?"

"No. I can't say that I have. Nothing better than guesses, and those not very probable."

"Well, you're getting on all the same. If you go on collecting facts, you're bound to get the complete puzzle at last, and the pieces fall into place."

Superintendent Davis made this somewhat platitudinous statement with more cheerfulness than the inspector felt to be justified by the event. His own feeling was that he had been blocked again, just as he had been hopeful that the solution to what he had begun to style mentally the Hamilton mystery was within his reach. But the explanation of this optimistic attitude came with the next sentence: "There's something else been happening while you've been busy about Addison's death. I thought I'd like to hear first what you'd got to report, but it seems that he wasn't the only one to get rattled over the discovery that you made on Friday. Addison decided that he'd better commit suicide, and North and Ada Hamilton thought their best chance was to bolt."

"You mean they've cleared out?"

"That's how it looks."

"It's the first bit of luck we've had in this case. It's what I should have asked them to do. They haven't a chance, of course. But how much start did they get?"

"About half an hour. It was like this: the Hamilton woman went back to Lobbs & Rider's this morning, as though nothing had happened. I suppose North arranged that—"

"No. It was her solicitor, Mr. Jellipot. He threatened Lobbs with a writ for libel unless he reinstated her."

"Jellipot? I thought he did a different class of business from that. It's the way to get struck off the rolls. She must be an infernally clever woman to get round a man of his age and experience. I wonder she ever got him to take the case."

"I don't think I should call her particularly clever. It was I who recommended her to him, as a matter of fact."

"Why did you do that?"

"Oh, she had to have someone. Besides, I didn't expect the case to develop quite as it has."

"Well, she went back as though she were going to settle down although that can only have been with the idea of diverting suspicion, and North also arrived at the office at about his usual time—a few minutes after herself. The man who had been watching her wasn't feeling well, and as it wasn't expected that either of them would come out again before midday, he telephoned to know whether he could come away and leave Reeves, who had North under observation, in sole charge. He asked to speak to you, and as you were out Thomson referred the matter to me, and I told him if he left Reeves watching the office it would be sufficient, at any rate till nearer midday.

"I am responsible for that, but I don't see what difference it would have made if they'd both been there.

"At about eleven-twenty they came out together. Reeves says that they both looked particularly well dressed, as though they'd been frugal-minded enough to decide to bolt in their best clothes, as they won't be likely to see the others again, whether they're caught or get clear.

"He says they walked straight over to him, where he was standing looking into a shop-window on the other side of the street, and North spoke to him as bold as brass, and asked him if he'd be good enough to stop following him about, as what was a joke at first became a bore if it were kept up too long. He said something about having a lady with him, and preferring to having a few hours to themselves, and that Reeves would be a wise man if he were to get some lunch and come back at a later hour.

"Reeves told him that the street was equally free for all, and that he'd got his duty to do, and that he was sorry, but he couldn't be taking orders from him.

"He says that the girl was plainly in a nervous, frightened condition, but the man seemed in good spirits, and ready to fly at anyone on a small provocation. It wasn't very surprising that he was feeling like that, considering the tricky plan that he must have had in mind all the time.

"Well, Reeves followed the two of them into Falk Street, thanking his luck that they didn't take separate ways, and saw them go into the Delincourt Garage there. He says he wasn't many paces behind, as there was no object in avoiding their observation after what North had said, and he wanted to see and hear all that he could.

"There was a Morris Minor standing at the curb, and the garage manager must have met them almost at the door as they went in, for the three came out together as Reeves came up, and the manager said: "Here it is, Mr. North. You'll find it's all ready to start," or something to that effect, showing that the whole thing was arranged, and the two got in in front, North taking the wheel.

"Reeves didn't feel much concerned. He thought if they were trying a getaway that they hadn't chosen the right car. But he'd got to learn that he was wrong about that.

"He stopped a taxi, and followed them not more than a dozen yards behind. When the road was clear, North drove up to about the thirty-mile limit, but he didn't seem to be making any attempt to shake Reeves off his track, and once when they were stopped by the red light, and pulled up side by side, he looked out through the open window, and asked Reeves whether the public knew that they had to pay for that sort of nonsense, and then turned to ask the driver which was the best road to take for Greenford. He said he expected the taxi-man knew the roads better than he did, and if they were going together they might just as well agree on the best way.

"The man took this as a joke, without quite knowing what to make of it, but he agreed with North as to what was the best road, and Reeves said he felt rather a fool, especially when the taxi drew ahead once or twice, and the Morris followed. So he stopped that, and they kept behind till Greenford was reached, and after that North seemed to know his road without asking anyone, as no doubt he did.

"He turned south for about a mile, and then gave the signal that he was about to turn to the left, and as the taxi, that was quite close behind, slowed down, North turned into a side-track that isn't meant for vehicles at all, but that leads through to another road two or three hundred yards away.

"There was a row of posts blocking it, but one of them had been broken down. Reeves says that it looked quite fresh, as though North himself might have done it the night before, but that doesn't sound very probable. It just gave the Morris Minor space to squeeze through, scraping the paint as you might say, but of course the taxi couldn't follow.

"Reeves says he told his driver to put on all the speed he could, and try to find a broader turning that would get him round the way they had gone, and so he did, but they never saw the Morris again, probably because he assumed that it would be heading away from London, and it looks as though they must have turned back."

Chief-Inspector Combridge had listened to his superior officer, up to this point, with a commendable restraint, though not without a feeling that he could have given the essential facts in about one-tenth of the time. Now he interrupted to ask: "I suppose he's got the number of the car?"

"Yes. He took that at the start. And there's no occasion for you to get restless, as though you want to jump up and run bare-headed about the streets looking for a Morris Minor that isn't there. You ought to know that everything in this office doesn't stop because you're out for a few hours.

"We've got every road watched, and if they abandon the car somewhere, as I think they're most likely to do, the chances are that it will be spotted in half an hour."

Inspector Combridge replied: "I expect that's what they'll do, all the same. They meant to drive back through London to get clear of pursuit, and then park the car somewhere—probably in one of the shopping streets where no one would give it a glance as they pull up—and then leave London another way. It's not badly planned, especially if they have the sense not to leave London at all."

He could afford to admire, with an untroubled mind, the simplicity of the manoeuvre by which Sergeant Reeves had been foiled, knowing that no ingenuity would be likely to secure more than forty-eight hours of liberty, which would be very dearly bought at the cost of a presumption of mutual conspiracy in flight, and probably in a common crime.

He would have placed the chance of Philip North getting away alone at something like five hundred to one, but that of the two together would be too small for calculation.

Already every policeman within a fifty miles radius would have become alertly watchful for such a pair: tomorrow the power of the Press would take their description to every home.

Already every main railway station, every coach terminus, every port of embarkation, would be watched. Their sole chance, such as it was, would be to remain in hiding among the millions of Greater London; and that chance would be negligible unless they had already provided themselves with separate identities which they could adopt without arousing the suspicions of those around them—an elaboration of precaution seldom attempted even by those who plot crime with deliberation, and particularly improbable here, where flight could have been no part of a programme in which they must stand their ground unsuspected to obtain the fortune for which they sinned.

"I suppose," the inspector went on, "I needn't ask whether you've enquired at the Delincourt Garage what North said when he hired the car (unless he bought it outright)? Not that that will tell us much, except we shall know one thing that we can rule out, as it will be sure not to be true."

"Yes, we've actually done that! The manager—that fellow Wheeler that we had up at the last sessions for smashing up two cyclists when he was testing a sports car. You remember how cleverly Campion bounced the jury to let him off—he says North ordered it by phone on Saturday morning, and rang up again that night to make sure that it would be ready punctually. He hired it for 'about four hours,' and confirmed this by a letter that arrived on Monday morning, with an open cheque for one pound as deposit enclosed."

"It wasn't much of a deposit."

"No. But it and the writing paper together established his identity, and gave the name of his bank, at which Wheeler could have had enquiry made by his own, if he had wished. Cars are hired every day quite as casually. I should say North showed his sense in not making more fuss over how it was done."

"Well, there's one thing more we can do before we decide what's to be said when we've got them under observation again, and that's to enquire what excuse they made when they walked out of Lobbs & Rider's together."

"Strange to say, that's been done too. Mr. Lobbs says that the girl turned up punctually, but seemed rather nervous, which wasn't surprising, any way of looking at it. She asked, almost as soon as she arrived, if he would mind if she just got things in order and left at mid-morning, and commenced in earnest tomorrow.

"He didn't make any difficulty about that. Perhaps he wasn't likely to under all the circumstances, but he says that she spent the next hour getting the place straight, according to the ways she'd been used to before she left, and if she really knew all the time that it was the last hour she'd have there he thinks she's about the best actress he ever met."

"Well, the women that come our way often are. Anything else?"

"Only that he also noticed how she was dressed. Not quite the usual office get-up, I suppose."

"What about North?"

"He told another partner—Ribblestone, or some such name—that he should be away for the day, and asked him to see a patient for him. But it appears that he hadn't made any later appointments for the day, although he had booked up as usual for the rest of the week. Of course, it would have aroused suspicion if he hadn't. It's evident that it had all been very carefully planned."

Inspector Combridge rose, with a feeling that the case was moving rapidly to its destined end. He said: "Well, there doesn't seem to be much more to be done till we have the pleasure of meeting them again.... Seeing that it's getting on for four, it's about time to think about having lunch.... I suppose there'll be no difficulty about warrants now?"

"I've settled that with Sir Henry just before you came in. They are both to be detained, and brought here for questioning, wherever they may be found.

"When we've had a little talk, and taken statements if possible, they are to be formally charged. Sir Henry thinks the evidence is quite sufficient for that."

"Yes, I suppose it is. Though there are still too many things that we don't know. I shouldn't care for the job of drawing the brief."

"Perhaps not, though I should say it would give you a worse headache to draw one for the defence. But we can leave the lawyers to that."

Inspector Combridge went without further reply in search of his needed meal.

"I wonder," he thought, with a stir of inward amusement, of which he should have been ashamed, as having been the one who had led Mr. Jellipot into the mess. "I wonder what Jellipot will say when he hears this!" He decided that, when be had attended to his more physical requirements, he would ring him up, and find out.

CHAPTER XXVIII.

"I SUPPOSE," Inspector Combridge began, "you haven't heard the latest news about Philip North and Miss Hamilton?"

"That," he heard Mr. Jellipot's voice with its usual careful intonation, and its exactness of matter, "must be a difficult question to answer until I am informed what the news may be."

"You haven't heard that they both bolted this morning?"

"No, I can't say that I had."

"Well, that's how it is. Led our man a dance this morning and gave him the slip by a trick that North must have thought out beforehand. They got the laugh of him all right, but there's a proverb about that, which they may remember before many hours are over."

"You mean that he laughs longest who laughs last? I always regard proverbs with suspicion, because there are so many that cancel each other out, but I will agree that that one sounds reasonable.... May I ask what you propose to do now?"

"Run them in, of course."

"I am sorry that you should feel it necessary to do that. Do you mean that you have decided definitely to charge them with Mrs. Hamilton's murder?"

"We shall certainly detain them both when they are found, which will be in the next few hours, more likely than not. I can't say what will be done about North till we've considered any statement he cares to make, but I think we've let the girl run loose rather too long already."

"You can't charge Ada Hamilton."

"Can't charge her? Why not? You don't mean she's committed suicide?"

"Not precisely. But you know I don't like discussing matters of this kind over the telephone. Why not come along now and talk it over?"

"But you said you didn't even know that they'd cleared out?"

POST-MORTEM EVIDENCE, BY S. FOWLER WRIGHT

"I endeavoured to answer with accuracy, but I can observe the possibility of having been misunderstood."

"I wish you'd say straight out what you mean."

"That is what I have been trying to do. Haven't I asked you to come along here, and clear up anything you don't understand?"

"Well, I'll come."

The tone of consent was ungracious, for the inspector felt that Mr. Jellipot was either fencing with him in a spirit of most inopportune levity, or concealing something of real importance in a manner not easy to accept with complacency. But he had nothing more urgent to do, the search for the missing couple not being a matter requiring his personal attention. And he felt a vague uneasiness as to what it might be that Mr. Jellipot knew, and which underlay that assurance—or was it not almost a threat?—that Ada Hamilton had passed beyond the reach of the law? Had North chartered a powerful plane in which they had taken off to some distant land? To some remote wilderness of the world where they hoped to avoid pursuit? Or to one of those few remaining countries where extradition treaties do not exist?

It seemed a most probable supposition, and would leave him to face the blame of having allowed her so long a liberty after her guilt had become evident to any reasonable man. It was true that the sole or ultimate responsibility was not his, but he knew that it would be laid at his door, and he would be expected to take it in. The fear hardened his resolution that, if he should get her in his sight again, he would allow nothing to move him to let her go.

He had some reduction of fear when he remembered that a plane suitable for such ocean flights would not easily be procured without a substantial payment, which would almost certainly be required in the form of cash in advance, and he knew that no steps had been taken as yet to put Ada Hamilton in possession of the fortune that came to her by her stepmother's death. But he was less informed as to what Philip North's available means might be, and there was warning in the ingenuity and determination he had already shown. Perhaps there was ground for a better hope in the improbability that either of the fugitives would be able to handle a plane. But one thing, at least, was sure—there was something that Mr. Jellipot knew, and which he had promised to tell.

Worried with these doubts, he was shown into the solicitor's office, to be greeted quietly with: "Well, Inspector, you haven't been long in coming!"

He observed, without satisfaction, that Mr. Jellipot seemed to be amused, as though aware of a secret joke, and yet with an almost nervous gravity, as though it were a joke that must be handled with doubt and care, lest it prove to be one which had been bought at a tragic price. He was certainly in no haste to talk, leaving it to Inspector Combridge to open the conversation.

"I understood that, if I came here at once, you'd have some information to give me."

"I believe what I actually said was that I would endeavour to elucidate any statement I had already made which you had been unable to understand."

"Well, I thought you talked as though you knew where they were hiding out. I don't think you'd be a party to concealing them from the law."

"No, you are right there. It would be against my duty as an officer of the court. It would also be an exceptionally silly thing to attempt. As a fact, unless you can tell me that you have warrants issued, the question does not arise. But let me ask you this. Suppose I should be able to tell you where they actually are, would you, in return for that information, promise me that you would do nothing hurriedly until the position has been fully discussed?"

Inspector Combridge hesitated. The price did not sound too high for the information that it would buy, but he had made one or two of these bargains before, and had a feeling that Mr. Jellipot was handling him in a way that he did not like. Might it not be better to go his own way, and effect the arrests without any troublesome conditions being attached thereto? The thought reminded him of Mr. Jellipot's statement that Ada Hamilton had already passed beyond the reach of the law. He said: "I thought you told me that Miss Hamilton was already out of our reach?"

"That is one of the matters which I am anxious to explain, if you will permit me to do so."

"Very well. I'm here to listen."

"Then I will consider the bargain made. Miss Ada Hamilton ceased to exist at or about 1:00 P.M. today."

"You mean she's committed suicide? That's what I asked you before."

"Combridge, I didn't think you could be so dull! She ceased to exist by becoming Mrs. Philip North, as I am sure you were aware that she was aiming to do."

"Then they haven't—you mean they haven't bolted at all?"

"No one except Sergeant Reeves has ever suggested that they had. The Morris Minor, the slimness of which caused him so much annoyance, was returned to the garage within the time for which it had been hired. I believe you can put a detective to shadow anyone without breaking any recognized law, but I am not aware that the object of these attentions is under any obligation to remain within the range of your supervision, if he consider privacy to be a preferable condition of life."

"I suppose you've known this all along?"

"No. I learnt of it little more than an hour ago. I may say that I should have advised against it with all the emphasis in my power."

"It does rather show up the motive that started them on the crime."

"You must please not attribute that line of argument to myself. My objection was entirely different. I think it may have increased my difficulty in discovering the truth of this rather singular case, which I had become hopeful that I should do."

"You mean you might have got Philip to blurt it out, to save his own skin, and you don't think they'll be got to give evidence against each other now?"

"No. I was thinking of something entirely different. But I believe North did put some idea of that kind before Miss Hamilton, to persuade her to this rather hurried development."

"Well, that's frank, anyway!"

"I prefer frankness wherever possible. As a matter of fact, as I have been reminded this afternoon, he commenced to consult me on the subject, but we were unfortunately interrupted, or I may say with some confidence that this marriage would not have occurred."

"And you tell me he did it so that he couldn't be called to give evidence against her?"

"I believe that was the idea which he put before her. But my dear Inspector, the complexity of human motives! The impetuosity of youth!"

"If that's all they were planning to do, I can't see why they needed to go to so much trouble to give Reeves the slip."

"Neither can I. It appears to have resulted from a most reasonable doubt in Miss Hamilton's mind concerning the soundness of the arguments which were urged upon her. She finally consented to the marriage on the express condition that it should take place without the knowledge of your excellent detective force."

"And you were to tell me about it the same afternoon?"

"No. I can assure you that neither of them anticipated that this interview would occur."

"And now I suppose you're going to tell me that they've gone honeymooning in Nova Zemblya or the Philippine Islands, and we're to please do nothing till they think it's time to come home and be hanged?"

"On the contrary, I was about to tell you that they are waiting in the next room.... And now that the position is sufficiently understood, I propose to ask them in, so that we may have the frank discussion you were good enough to promise."

Inspector Combridge felt that his memory of that promise was indistinct, but it was clearly a position in which a little patience could do no harm—except to those unfortunate couples who were being stopped and questioned by zealous constables in various parts of the area of Greater London—and he remained silently seated, and even gave a grunt of recognition, as the two suspects entered the room, and the solicitor said: "Here are Mr. and Mrs. Philip North," with a lightness of tone which was partially successful in concealing his real anxiety as to how that interview would be likely to terminate.

CHAPTER XXIX.

"WHAT I ask you to do, Inspector," Mr. Jellipot said, with an unusual earnestness of voice and manner, "is to put all previous assumptions out of your mind, and to discuss this matter for half an hour—I will not ask for longer than that—on the basis that my clients are actually innocent, and that an alternative explanation must therefore exist, and should not be beyond human ingenuity to discover."

He looked at the inspector, who was in no haste to respond. He said at last: "I don't know that my imagination would be quite equal to that. I don't want to be rude, but I'm not going to let you lead me down the garden again."

"I am afraid that your meaning is clearer than the picturesque metaphor which you have selected for its communication. May I assure you that I have no such intention? I have been of some service in introducing you to these young people, who might not have been easy to find if I had adopted an opposite course, and in return I ask you for half an hour."

"You make it very awkward when you put it like that. Of course, I'll listen to anything, but I don't think this is where it ought to be said, and I ought to caution them first. It's no use blinking the fact that I shall have to ask them to come with me."

"Inspector," Mr. Jellipot went on stubbornly, though with a diminishing hope which rendered it increasingly difficult to maintain the tone he desired, "you are married, and I believe at least as happily as you deserve. It is a matter of which I cannot speak from experience, but I am sure that you would not have liked to end the day of your marriage locked up in a separate cell. It is surely a position in which you can at least—"

Inspector Combridge interrupted with an unusual display of irritation. "It's no use talking like that. It's no use asking me to be sentimental. I've got my duty to do."

He saw the edge of the pit of weakness on which he stood. He saw Ada North's hand trembling on the arm of the chair upon which it lay. Why couldn't women who commit murders of the meanest kind look different from more decent girls? He remembered an occasion years before when he had been talked over in such a matter, and had had to offer his resignation in consequence, though it had not been accepted. If he should be weak now, would he be likely to be firmer in half an hour?

He rose resolutely, and as he did so, the telephone rang.

He heard Mr. Jellipot say: "Yes, he's here." And then: "We are in the midst of an important conference. Unless it be of a most urgent importance, I should prefer—you mean it's—wait a moment, please."

He covered the mouth of the receiver to say: "Inspector, it's your superintendent on the phone. He wants to speak to you. It's something about this matter, that he thinks you should know. If you speak, will you promise me that you will not tell him, for the moment at least, that my clients are with you here?"

"No. I can't promise anything. You must leave that for me to judge." He took the receiver from Mr. Jellipot's reluctant hand. They heard him say: "Yes. Combridge speaking," and after that there were three endless minutes of silence, broken only by an occasional monosyllabic exclamation or assent. It seemed that the superintendent must have a good deal to say. But at last the inspector said: "Well, it's a good thing we know. We might have had the public watching us bark under the wrong tree. But it doesn't clear anything, does it? It makes the fog a bit worse than it was before." And after a further moment of silence he said: "Oh, by the way, I shall have something more to report when I come in. You can call off the search.... Yes, I know where they are.... I'll be back within an hour. I can't explain on the phone."

He laid the instrument down, and they heard him say "Damn!" under his breath. He looked at Mr. Jellipot as he continued more audibly: "You win. You can have the half an hour you want, and see what you can do to make me a bigger fool than I am now. I oughtn't to resign. I ought to be kicked out."

"It is a concession," Mr. Jellipot answered gratefully, "which I am sure you will not regret, and I must be careful not to lose the short time that your consideration allows. But if the information you have just had bears on this matter, as I understood was the case, may I ask whether it is something that you can let us know?"

"Yes. It's only right that you should. A dentist—a man named Hassell—has been to the yard to say that he bought a quantity of the drug from Dr. Addison last week. The quantity agrees with that which was missing, and the presumption is—it's only fair to say this—that it was Dr. Addison who had taken it, to increase an otherwise inadequate income at the expense of the firm who employed him.

"Hassell says that he's bought most of his drugs from Addison during the last few years, and had no suspicion that anything was wrong. He thought that Addison got them more cheaply in large quantities than a single dentist would be able to do.

"He heard rumours of the enquiry which was being made about this drug, and then of Dr. Addison's suicide, and he very properly thought that he ought to report his transactions with him.

"It's easy to see now why Addison took his own life. He knew his dishonesty must come out, unless he were prepared to let suspicion fall in the wrong direction, which it might—indeed, it would—have been impossible to do, as Mr. Hassell's action has shown, even if he had been willing to save his reputation at such a cost; so I suppose he chose to confess in his own way.

"Where I blame myself most is that I had Hassell's name, with that of two or three other dentists, under my own eyes, on a sheet of paper that had some notes or figures that didn't appear to have any particular significance—I don't suppose he meant them to be comprehensible to anyone under whose eyes they might happen to fall—but I've no doubt now that they were the names and addresses of the dentists with whom he dealt, and memoranda of his transactions with them.

"I've no doubt I should have tumbled to what they were if I hadn't got my own theory of what had happened fixed in my mind, and been looking solely for anything that could give me light on Mrs. Hamilton's death."

"I think," Mr. Jellipot answered, recognizing the generosity of the inspector's admission, especially in the hearing of those whom he had been too quick to condemn, "that it was a very natural conclusion to which you had come. But the information you have received is particularly opportune, because I was going to ask you to accept the possibility of such an explanation, and I am conscious that you may consider my suggestions to be sufficiently improbable on quite separate grounds."

The reply reminded the inspector of the difficulty of the position in which he stood, and of his resolution of a few minutes before that he would not allow any sentimental weakness to cause him to deviate from duty's unpleasant path. The case against Mrs. Hamilton's stepdaughter still seemed to him to be too simply convincing to be set aside by any ingenious theory which must be described in advance as of a "sufficiently improbable" kind. Let Mr. Jellipot produce an alternative murderer, a motive equally strong, an access to the new drug equally simple, and they would then have something of which to talk, even though the writer of the anonymous letters might still be missing. But he was well assured that this could not be done.

Wishing to avoid expectations which were not likely to be realized, he expressed this opinion with a blunt directness which Mr. Jellipot, who was of a recovered equanimity now that he had secured the inspector's promise to listen, received apparently unperturbed.

"I am not proposing," he replied quietly, "to offer you either a murderer, or a motive, or an access to any drug. I am going to suggest to you the probability that Mrs. Hamilton died an absolutely natural death."

CHAPTER XXX.

"I'M afraid," Inspector Combridge said, "you'll have a hard job to make me believe that. You've got the letter first, which shows that someone knew what was wrong, even if we can't find out who it is, and then you've got Sir Lionel spotting the drug, and two independent analysts proving that he'd made the right guess If you could get any jury to bring in a verdict of natural causes in face of that—!"

"Even that might not be impossible. I suppose the simplest way would be to engage a larger number of expert witnesses to swear something different."

"I don't say you couldn't do that. But I thought you'd got something you were going to ask me to really believe. You're not going to say that Sir Lionel made a bad guess, and then two other doctors found the same thing, though it wasn't there?"

"Not at all. I have, in fact, no doubt that it was. The whole theory of what occurred hangs upon that. The question is, how long had it been where it was found?"

"I'm afraid I don't follow you."

"It is a question of logical deduction in the first place, and then of a theory that will fit the facts."

"Well, go on. I'll try not to interrupt again."

"I ask you to consider the case as it would appear if you were entirely certain that Miss—Mrs North is entirely innocent, which is my personal conviction, though I will own"—he glanced apologetically at Ada as he said this—"there was a time when I was not equally sure.

"What is the position, on that assumption? We have two eminent analysts finding a rare drug, difficult to procure, in the organs submitted to their tests. Were they both honestly mistaken? It is highly improbable. Did they both lie? It is more improbable still. Putting, for the time, these possibilities aside, for examination only as a final resort, we may conclude that the drug was there.

"We are then faced with the question of how or when it could have been introduced. Here Dr. Burfoot naturally comes under the first and strongest suspicion. He had ample opportunity. He could have obtained the poison. But, in fact, it appears that—at least directly or by any known channel—he did not do so.

"For that, and other reasons which I need not detail, I was disposed to pass Dr. Burfoot, and consider other possibilities.

"The household domestics were dismissed more easily. Knowledge of, or access to the drug, or any adequate motive—the idea was without plausibility of any kind.

"And at this point it became necessary to observe that I had been obsessed by an assumption that was absolutely illogical. I had assumed, because the analysts discovered a certain drug in the organs that were submitted to them, that it must have been present when death occurred. But when I faced the question, I observed that there was no evidence of this whatever. Dr. Burfoot had attributed death, without hesitation, to another adequate cause.

"Who, if anyone, had come into contact with those organs after death, who also had access to this drug which was so difficult to procure?

"There is one obvious answer. Sir Lionel Tipshift, on his own admission, had been concerned in experiments which had familiarized him with its effects, and which, if his evidence is to be believed, had enabled him to recognize its presence when it was beyond the detection of the ordinary professional eye."

"You mean," Inspector Combridge broke the exemplary silence with which he had received these surprising conclusions to ask incredulously, "that the whole thing may have been an accident in Sir Lionel's laboratory, or wherever the post-mortem was held?"

"No. It would be a possible theory, but for the existence of the anonymous letter, which appears to render it improbable, whereas there are no more than superficial aspects of improbability in that which I am putting before you."

"If Mrs. Hamilton died of natural causes, and the drug got into the organs subsequently, I don't see how that explains the letter, whether it was by accident, or in any other way."

"That, if you will pardon me saying so, arises from the natural difficulty of discussing a theory which you have not heard."

"Well, go ahead. I'll try not to interrupt, as I said before. If you've got a theory that shows up who wrote the letter, I'll say there's something we can get our teeth into. You won't take me far without that."

"I am sorry that you are unwilling to leave me to state the premises of my contention in an orderly manner. But the letter was obviously written by Vincent Hamilton."

"You mean he'd plotted to plant a murder on Miss Hamilton that she hadn't done, so that she would be hanged, and he'd get the estate? Well, I shouldn't doubt that he'd be equal to that."

"But I should. I don't think that he is of the nature to attempt such a crime, and I don't think he did. I think his plan was much more subtle and complicated, and intended to reach a quite different end. If I am right, it was the kind of plot which he finds pleasure in working out, with novel features of criminality, such as those with which he has annoyed you at least once already."

"Well, if you've got a scheme for putting salt on Vincent Hamilton's tail, you'll find everyone at the Yard will be willing to lend a hand. If we don't believe you, it won't be for lack of a good try."

"But that is more than I may be able to do."

"You mean he's going to get away with it again?"

"No. I think his scheme has already failed—finally and utterly failed, and I am rather anxious to know what line he will take when he hears the news, as he must in the next few hours, even if he doesn't learn it from me.

"It is that doubt which decided me before you came in that I must try to persuade you at once of what I believe to be the truth, which I might otherwise have left until further developments had made it an easier matter to undertake.

"Vincent's anticipations went wrong on one vital point. He assumed that suspicion would fall so strongly upon Miss Hamilton that Mr. North's first anxiety would be to dissociate himself from her, and from any possible suggestion of complicity in the crime which he would believe she had committed. He was right about the degree of suspicion that would arise. He was only wrong in his estimate of Mr. North's reaction to it. But that error has proved fatal to the purpose he had in view. The event was to result in a marriage, but it was to be that of Miss Hamilton and himself."

"Well," Inspector Combridge conceded, "it sounds likely enough, so far as Hamilton is concerned; but I don't see how anything could have been done without Sir Lionel's complicity, and I suppose you'll scarcely ask me to believe that he connived at the plot?"

"Why not?" The direct brevity of the question, asked with a curtness which was not Mr. Jellipot's usual manner, disconcerted the inspector for a moment. The reasons seemed to him to be too apparent for any explanation to be required. "His character and position," he answered. "His public position—"

"He was appointed to that position on the ground that he was a surgeon who had won reputation as a skilful analyst, and presumably also because he is an expert witness who has a most plausible and convincing manner, the authority of which is illogically increased by the knighthood which was subsequently bestowed upon him. His character, except in the negative sense that he had not, prior to the date of his appointment, been involved in any open scandal, probably did not enter into the question at all.

"To say that, is not to conclude that it may not have been of the most exemplary pattern. It is simply to observe that his part in the event should be examined with the same open-minded willingness to discover opportunities or indications of wrongdoing that would be applied, shall I say to Mr. and Mrs. North?"

"But the entire absence of motive—"

"—is an assumption which further enquiry may clear away. Will you allow me to reconstruct the event as I suppose that it occurred?"

"We commence with the fact—about which I think there is no doubt—that Vincent Hamilton desired to marry his cousin Ada, whether from natural attraction or cupidity it is needless to determine. He was rejected, Miss Hamilton inclining very wisely to prefer Mr. North, whom she has now decisively chosen.

"Vincent, as we know, is a man who is ingenious to obtain his ends, and hindered by few scruples in the methods which he employs. He resolved to devise some method which would discredit Mr. North, and restore him to favour.

"Mrs. Hamilton was ill, and her death was not unlikely at any time. Either in anticipation of that event, or, and perhaps more probably, immediately upon its occurrence, Vincent contrives an ingenious plot, the first step of which is the anonymous letter which reached the coroner on the day of the funeral, on which he hesitated to act.

"Nothing becoming public during the days immediately following, Vincent becomes restless, as everything depends upon the coroner having been roused to action, and telephones him from Piccadilly Circus, to make sure that his first shot has not been a misfire.

"Meanwhile, he has arranged with Sir Lionel that the post-mortem, which will come under his hands in the expected routine, shall show evidence of poisoning, such as will inevitably throw suspicion upon Miss Hamilton, both as the one who nursed the deceased, and who will substantially benefit by her death."

"That"—Inspector Combridge could not restrain himself from interrupting again, as Mr. Jellipot allowed himself the instant's pause which this dramatic climax in the process of his imagination appeared to require—"is the point at which an otherwise plausible theory appears to me to approach fantastic improbabilities. What conceivable hold could Vincent Hamilton have upon Sir Lionel Tipshift to induce him to engage in so grave, and—from his point of view—so needless a crime? It must be extremely improbable that they could have been even distantly acquainted, and beyond reasonable supposition that any friendly intimacy could have existed between them. Is it likely that Vincent Hamilton, having devised such a plot, would then find himself able to obtain the co-operation of the one man who could enable it to succeed?"

"No. It would be grotesquely improbable, and we may therefore conclude with some confidence that it did not occur in that way. It would be more in accordance with the usual course of human imaginations to suppose that a previous contact with Sir Lionel, with the knowledge that he had the means to influence him, first suggested the scheme to Vincent Hamilton's mind.... By the way, Inspector, do you know what Sir Lionel Tipshift's recreations are?"

"No," Inspector Combridge answered frankly. "I should have supposed him to be absorbed in his professional and experimental work."

"Then I can add to your knowledge that he is a heavy and unsuccessful gambler, and is consequently in the hands of money-lenders, who could, at any moment, ruin his public reputation, if they should elect to do so.

"I owe the first piece of knowledge to the action of Vincent Hamilton—deliberately taken, as I have since thought, with that object—and the second to enquiries which I have made during the last twenty-four hours through a firm of solicitors, who are under certain obligations to me, and whose business lies largely among the money-lending fraternity.

"I may add that Vincent Hamilton also gave me an opportunity of observing that Sir Lionel is not a stranger to his acquaintance, though I formed the opinion that, on one side at least, it was an unwelcome intimacy."

"Well," the inspector conceded, as Mr. Jellipot paused again, "I'll allow that you've found out more than one thing that we ought to look at rather closely, but, if all this were true, I don't see how the thing could be expected to end.

"You say that Vincent meant to marry Miss Hamilton—presumably when suspicion had been removed. And it isn't easy to see how that could be without exposing what Sir Lionel had done, and you won't ask me to believe that he'd ever have agreed to that."

"Obviously not. But is it not at least possible that Vincent had cast Sir Lionel for a part of which he was unaware, and which was to be the final twist which would delight the perverse ingenuity of his somewhat exceptional mind? I mean that the scheme, so far as Sir Lionel would be aware, would end with the condemnation of Miss Hamilton for a crime she had not committed, the consequent passing of her father's fortune into Vincent's hands, and the paying over of the agreed proportion which would enable Sir Lionel to discharge or reduce his debts. But Vincent would have carried it on—perhaps by the means of further anonymous letters, but that is a mere guess—to a different end, involving Sir Lionel's exposure, and his own marriage to Miss Hamilton, who would thus show her gratitude to a loyal lover, and enable him to acquire control of her fortune without the disadvantage of having to share it with another man."

Inspector Combridge listened to this theory of a murder which had not occurred, with the feelings of one who fights against some overwhelming mesmeric influence, which will and reason reject, but which is still forcing itself upon his subjective mind.

"I don't know whether you've realized," he said stubbornly, "that your theory makes Tipshift out to be an almost impossible monster. If it were only a matter of faking a bit of evidence to complete a case that wasn't easy to prove, I don't say that he mightn't oblige, even under rather less pressure than you suggest may have been applied, but it's a different thing to have someone hanged for a crime which you know hasn't happened at all."

"I am pleased," Mr. Jellipot observed placidly, "to observe that we are in substantial agreement upon a theory which I have put forward with some diffidence, and not without recognition of the possibility that I may be entirely wrong."

"Well," exclaimed the astonished inspector, "if you can tell me how you make that out! What I tried to say was—"

"The argument you employed," Mr. Jellipot answered, in his quietest manner, which he had now fully resumed, as though having become aware that the stress of conflict was past, "is one that can be answered without difficulty, and I venture to think in a conclusive manner. But there was a greater significance in your allusion to Sir Lionel Tipshift, the eminent and titled surgeon, by the indignity of his surname only. It showed that you had subconsciously removed him from the respectable and law-abiding sections of the community to that of the criminal population. You may have observed that even the Press will hesitate to make this distinction until after committal, and will sometimes retain the ordinary courtesies of respect until the trial of an accused person be advanced to its second day."

"I can't say that I have, but I should be more interested to hear the conclusive answer that is so easy to give."

"Which you shall certainly have. The real distinction which you are attempting to draw is not between human actions of ordinary or monstrous character, but simply between usual and unusual crimes.

"You were ready to suppose that Miss Hamilton would plot the death of another woman with whom she was living on terms of intimacy and trust, with no more object than to obtain earlier control of money which she did not urgently need, and which would have ultimately come to her hands in an innocent way.

"Yet you are startled and repelled by the suggestion that Sir Lionel Tipshift should be guilty of an action which is intended to consign a woman to death, although she was an absolute stranger to him, and his whole career and reputation might be at stake.

"Yet I will venture to assert that you knew nothing about Miss Hamilton to suggest that she was either of the character or disposition to design and execute so monstrous a crime; whereas you knew Sir Lionel Tipshift as a—shall I say a hardy—professional witness, and as an active vivisectionist, which is to say, at the least, that he is willing to subject his fellow-creatures to living torture, either in curious pursuit of knowledge, or in the belief—perhaps quite honestly held—that he is benefiting mankind by the ruthless experiments which he undertakes. If he will commit such acts for the vague expectation of benefiting his fellow men, is it particularly incredible that he would consign any one woman to death, when his own reputation and career should be the stake at issue?"

"That," Inspector Combridge conceded, "may sound reasonable enough, and, if we look at it in an unprejudiced way, I dare say that it's no less likely that Sir Lionel" (Mr. Jellipot noticed, with an excusable smile, that he was careful not to call him Tipshift again) "might commit such a crime than anyone else, and perhaps more so than some. But I'm sure you'll agree that there's a wide gap between saying that a man might have done such a thing, and proving he did."

"That," Mr. Jellipot replied, with careful deliberation, "is a proposition with which all of us here are likely to most emphatically agree."

CHAPTER XXXI.

CHIEF-INSPECTOR COMBRIDGE'S mind was not of a density which could fail to understand the implication of Mr. Jellipot's ready assent to the two-edged proposition which he had himself put forward.

He sat some time in a silence which neither the solicitor nor his clients appeared to be in any hurry to break, while he endeavoured to resolve an irresolute mind as to the attitude which he should adopt toward the startling possibility which Mr. Jellipot had so persuasively put before him.

It appeared to him that he must either accept it as an hypothesis requiring serious investigation, or else reject it with the logical consequence that he must subject Mr. Jellipot's clients to the arrest which most people (and especially those who have been married during the day) would much prefer to avoid. Under the influence of Mr. Jellipot's persuasive periods, he had been half-disposed to concede the possibility that his ingenious theory might supply the solution to what he had always admitted to be an unsatisfactory and perplexing case; but when he endeavoured to marshal the solicitor's arguments in his own mind, and imagined himself capitulating them to doubtful or derisive colleagues, he felt that he would incur their certain criticism, and the probable censure of his superiors, for having been turned aside from the arrests which it had been his clear duty to make, by a suggestion fantastic in itself, and destitute of any supporting evidence, such as would endure the cold light of a court of law.

He saw also that Mr. Jellipot's argument was as two-edged as his own. The solicitor had asked him to assume Miss Hamilton's innocence, and to accept the only alternative which, on that assumption, could be logically deduced from established facts. But if that alternative should be regarded as too absurd for serious credence, then its rejection must re-establish the earlier theory of Ada Hamilton's guilt in augmented strength.

"The suggestion you have made," he said at last, "is one that, I need scarcely say, will be the subject of most careful enquiry, and I may add that, for more reasons than one, I should be glad to find that you have set the right key in the lock; but you can scarcely dispute that it is, at present, no more than a conjecture, improbable in itself, and unsupported by any proof; and, in the meantime, I have no possible alternative but to take Mr. and Mrs. North back with me to Scotland Yard."

"Where they will in all probability be detained? Wait a moment, Mr. North, please."

Between his own anger, and the sight of Ada's distress, as it appeared to them that the new and hope-inspiring theory to which they had listened had been impotent to delay their arrest, Philip North, who up to now had maintained the silence and restraint to which he had pledged himself before the arrival of the inspector, was now, as Mr. Jellipot had been alert to observe, upon the edge of an explosion which might have sacrificed the last hope of a battle which even yet might not be entirely lost.

Now he controlled himself to no more than a muttered curse, as he heard the answer: "I'm afraid there's not much doubt about that."

Inspector Combridge rose as he spoke, but Mr. Jellipot turned to Ada without appearing to notice that significant movement.

"I suppose," he said, "you have not yet made the appointment with Vincent that was promised when you were here last week?"

"No, I told you it wouldn't be till after today."

"I believe you indicated it rather less definitely than that. I suppose he will not have heard of your marriage yet?"

"No, no one has."

"Inspector, if I have a few words with Vincent Hamilton on the phone in the outer office, will you mind listening in on this instrument?"

Inspector Combridge appreciated the delicacy of a proposal which would leave him in the company of his prisoners rather than to require him to retire to the outer room, but he looked sceptical of the utility of the suggestion.

"You surely don't think you're going to get any admission from him on the phone?" he asked. "Of course, I'd be glad enough to listen in if you could."

"I think it is no more than a poor hope, especially in view of what I shall have to tell him, but, with your consent, I propose to try."

"Suppose he says something that does you more harm than good?"

"It is a risk I am ready to take."

Without waiting for the possibility of further objections, Mr. Jellipot left the office, and Inspector Combridge, muttering a criticism of the solicitor's pertinacity, in which he compared him to a dog worrying a dry bone, a mild witticism for which he could scarcely anticipate applause from his present audience, took up the telephone.

He heard Mr. Jellipot put through to the Raleigh, and then a short interval while a search was being made for Vincent Hamilton, giving him time to consider the probability that he might be absent from the hotel, and to resolve that he would not allow that position to be made excuse for further delay, but after that he heard: "Yes, is that Mr. Jellipot speaking?" and became alert to listen to the conversation that followed.

"I have rung you up," Mr. Jellipot commenced, "on behalf of Miss Ada Hamilton, to apologize for the short delay which has occurred in making the appointment which you were good enough to promise, and to explain how it has occurred. I suppose you will not have already heard of today's event?"

"Haven't heard anything yet. You're not going to tell me that that red-headed flatfoot has run her in?"

"Not actually yet, though it is the imminence of that eventuality which is the immediate occasion of my anxiety to get into contact with you."

"I've said all along that she can bank on me for anything I'm able to do."

"So I had told her, and I can assure you that the offer was very warmly appreciated. The event which has preoccupied her attention today is one which I am sure you will recognize as a sufficient distraction to explain her silence. She has, in fact, become Mrs. Philip North."

"What?"

"She was married very quietly to Mr. North at midday today."

"Devils in hell!"

The expletive was followed by a moment's silence, which Mr. Jellipot did not break, and then Vincent Hamilton went on: "Well, that bursts it. I should have thought she'd have had more sense. I should like to know how she thinks he's going to get her out of the mess she's in."

"She doesn't think anything of the kind. She naturally relies upon me for that, and I may say that I am relying on you.... You see, I've got Mr. and Mrs. North and Inspector Combridge all here in my office together, and I've been trying to make the inspector see that there wasn't any murder at all."

"I should say you'll have a hard job to do that now."

"So I have found. It made me wonder whether you would answer one question, which might make all the difference to what I shall be able to do."

"I'm afraid not. Inspector Combridge and I are not really friends. Anyway, as things are now, you must count me out."

"I'm sure you don't really mean that. I have relied—"

"I'm not going to get mixed up with Combridge's crowd for you, or Ada, or anyone else. It isn't reasonable to ask."

"I don't think you will find me ask anything unreasonable, and I shan't ask you to help me without a fair *quid pro quo*. Suppose you let me put the proposition before you decline. I want you to give me just one question that I can ask Sir Lionel Tipshift that he won't like answering, and I will both give you my word of honour that you'll not be brought into it in any way, and will undertake that the Wall action shall be settled without further trouble or expense to yourself."

There was another pause of silence, during which it might be supposed that Vincent Hamilton was thinking hard. The inspector, listening intently for the next words, endeavoured to memorize with accuracy and assess the significance of those he had already heard. Vague and inconclusive as the conversation had been, it had yet contained implications that he knew must be deeply probed before he could pursue the case against Ada North in the simplicity of the original form in which it had been constructed. But what right had Mr. Jellipot to pledge his word of honour for the immunity of that which would be spoken in the very hearing of the police? Even in such an emergency as this, and to entrap a criminal such as Vincent Hamilton, it was something which, if he had not heard, he would not have believed that Jellipot would descend to do. Anyway, if he thought he could talk him over to agree to that, he would find, for once, that he had gone rather too far. His reflections were checked abruptly as Vincent's voice came again over the wire.

"Well, you're a sporting old bird. I suppose if I ask your legal advice you'll tell me not to trust any promise that's not in writing, and not much then that's not stamped and sealed; but I'm not such a mug that I don't know better than that. And what's done's done, and I can't say that I want Ada to swing. You can ask that dirty dog-chopper how he hopes to meet Fildes & Frobisher's bill for two thousand pounds next August. Drop it on him with a jerk when he's

186

giving evidence about how cleverly he could see poison that wasn't there, and you'll be able to watch him blink."

"I am much obliged to you, Mr. Hamilton. I may conclude that anonymous letters will now cease?"

"Sorry. I can't hear. I think there's something wrong with the wire."

Inspector Combridge heard the click of disconnection, and laid down the receiver. He looked at the two who had come so near to spending their separate nights in the accommodation which Scotland Yard provides for invited guests, and who had waited in ignorance of the conversation on which the last hope of liberty hinged.

"So far as I am concerned," he said, "you are free to go as you will, providing only that you will keep Mr. Jellipot informed of your address, so that we can get in touch with you, if necessary."

As he spoke, Mr. Jellipot re-entered the room. "I trust," he said, "that you will have experienced no difficulty in concluding that Sir Lionel Tipshift's financial difficulties had more influence upon the evidence which he gave than the condition of Mrs. Hamilton's body when the exhumation was made."

"I think," Inspector Combridge replied, with a grimness which may not have been lessened by a passing memory of Vincent Hamilton's irreverent allusion to the red-headed flatfoot, which he easily understood to be his own description, "that we shall have some questions to ask them both. But what I can't understand is how you could have promised Hamilton that you'd keep him out of the mess, when you knew I was listening to every word."

"It was, perhaps," Mr. Jellipot replied easily, "less a promise, though it may have been verbally in that form, than an intelligent anticipation of the event. Actually, there was singularly little of self-confession in what he said. I thought that he showed considerable powers of discrimination, and of transmitting ideas without the clumsiness of the spoken word."

"He made it quite clear that Sir Lionel, to his own knowledge, had had a bigger hand in the game than his official duty required, and he gave us a straight tip as to why it was done. I don't say I should have seen it with equal clearness if you hadn't given me some pointers before, but he wouldn't have talked as he did if he hadn't known some things that I'll own that I hadn't guessed, and if he hadn't tumbled to it that you'd worked them out to the right result."

"That," Mr. Jellipot replied, "was what I meant him to do.... But if you think I made a promise I cannot keep, it is an opinion which, if I may suggest it without offence, you will be most likely to change."

"I'm not going to let Vincent Hamilton off again, if you mean that."

"I mean that, for reasons of public policy, apart from other considerations, you will find that the Home Secretary will decline to authorize criminal proceedings against Sir Lionel Tipshift, unless he shall find himself obliged to do so, and if you can tell me how such proceedings can be taken against Hamilton separately, it will be something to learn.

"I venture to forecast that nothing but a scandal already published would induce the Home Office to institute a prosecution which would discredit the actual testimony on which several dozens of suspected murderers have been hanged within recent years, and the kind of testimony on which it will rely for the securing of future convictions.

"As that publicity depends entirely upon my own silence—for you must obey the directions of your department, and our friends here did not hear what was said—you may agree, upon further thought, that I gave no more explicit assurance than is justified by the position as I conceived it to be."

"Well, we won't argue that. I expect you'll be right again. But there'll be no man in London who'll have more need than Vincent Hamilton to be watching his step from now on.... I'd better get back and report. I don't suppose you'll be sorry to see me go."

He shook hands cordially enough with Mr. Jellipot and his intended prey, and the solicitor was left alone with the clients whom he had saved from a peculiarly inopportune detention, and probably from a most sinister sequel. He said: "No, you needn't waste time thanking me. If I hadn't always been rather a muddler, I might have cleared it up a bit sooner, and saved you both from an unpleasant afternoon. You acted in an exceptionally silly way, and the only thing that saved you was that you lost no time in coming to let me know what had happened.... As I'm under a promise to produce you if required, may I ask what you are proposing to do now?"

"Philip," Ada answered for both, "is coming home with me tonight, and we were intending to go back to Corbin Street in the morning, so that no one would know we were married except ourselves."

"Well, you can do better than that now. I have a client who visits Brighton occasionally, and who has spoken with approbation of the accommodation at the Two Queens Hotel. There is still time for Mrs. North to go back and pack whatever she may require, and for you to meet at Victoria, from which station the service is, I have been informed, of a rapid and frequent character. And meanwhile, with your permission, I will telephone the hotel for suitable accommodation to be reserved.... Yes, yes. It is very good of you to say so. But you may change your opinions when you know that you will be poorer, perhaps by as much as five hundred pounds, by what I have undertaken for you this afternoon, though I have some hope that I may compromise for a smaller sum.... But you can do me no greater favour now than to leave me free to attend to matters which have fallen very much in arrears during the past week."

Mr. Jellipot shook hands with an aspect of hurried and rather nervous cordiality, and turned back to a loaded desk.

APPENDIX A

Abstracted from a paragraph in the "Morning Standard" (May 17th*, 19—) headed*—"Unexpected Resignation of Sir Lionel Tipshift."

"...This sudden decision is understood to be due to the serious illness of Lady Tipshift, whose health has been a cause of some anxiety during the last two years. She has been advised that a long sea voyage is imperatively necessary, with subsequent wintering in a warmer climate."

APPENDIX B

Concluding words of a statement signed by Sir Lionel Tipshift, and filed in the office of Sir Forbes Petterton, K.C.B., Permanent Under-Secretary of State:

"—and I admit that I have been clearly warned that, in the event of my taking any office or place of public appointment or profit, either at home or abroad, the contents of this document will be communicated to the responsible quarters concerned."

ABOUT THE AUTHOR

SYDNEY FOWLER WRIGHT (1874-1965) penned over seventy volumes of science fiction, fantasy, classic mysteries, historical novels, poetry, and non-fiction, many of them being published by the Borgo Press Imprint of Wildside Press.